SUSAN PULLS THE STRINGS

SUSAN PULLS THE STRINGS

by
JANE SHAW

THE CHILDREN'S PRESS
LONDON AND GLASGOW

CONTENTS

CHAPTER ONE

CHANGES

SUSAN was doing her homework. And doing it rather well too, she thought complacently, drawing a line under the theorem that she had just proved. "I quite like geometry," she thought. "If you have a decent point on your pencil. And algebra's not bad. But I don't like arithmetic—"

Susan's mother was sitting over by the fire. She was doing the mending, but that her mind wasn't on it was obvious from the way that she kept glancing across at Susan. When she saw Susan leaning back and regarding her work with her head on one side and rather an air of conscious triumph, she said, "Have you nearly finished your homework, Susan?"

"I *have* finished," said Susan and began to put her books away in her case.

Her mother put down the sock that she was darning. "Susan," she said, "you know that Daddy's going to Africa to build that bridge?"

"Yes," said Susan. Naturally she knew that, considering that the Lyle household had talked about practically nothing else since Mr. Lyle, who was an engineer, had been given the job.

"Yes, well," said Mrs. Lyle, "I'm going with him."

Susan looked up. "Me too?" she said hopefully.

"I'm afraid not," said her mother. "No, darling, you could hardly have a year's holiday just now. Daddy and I have arranged for you to go to Uncle Charles in London—you'd like that, wouldn't you, with Charlotte and Midge and Bill?"

"Oh, *yes*," cried Susan, "I'd like that!" To go and live with the Carmichaels! Susan couldn't have imagined a happier arrangement. And in London too, the focus of all her dreams of adventures and excitements! And she hadn't been to London for ages, not since she was about ten—just a child. Besides, she doted on these cousins, who were lively and clever and beautiful —at least Charlotte, who was sixteen, and Bill, who was ten, were terribly good-looking, tall and golden-haired with big brown eyes and dark lashes of a ridiculous length. Susan herself was dark-haired and rosy-cheeked, and she admired particularly the looks of these fair cousins of hers. Margery, always known as Midge, was Susan's own age, and at the moment was a skinny little thing, all eyes in a small pointed face. People looking at her would nod knowingly and say that she would surprise them all one day and be the beauty of the family yet, but in the meantime she looked like—well, like a midge, Susan thought.

Their mother had died when Bill was quite small, and they were looked after by Aunt Lucy, who was Uncle Charles's sister and also Mrs. Lyle's sister, and who was considered by her nieces and nephew to be a pretty ancient person, but who was really only about thirty-seven or so at this time. Uncle Charles was a doctor, always busy, always on the run, and his family were always complaining that they saw nothing of him; but as Charlotte and Midge were at boarding-school that was scarcely surprising. Bill was a day-boy at his prep school.

"But, Mummy," Susan said, coming out of a happy dream, "what about school? I mean, here I am at school in Glasgow and I'm going to live in London—not very convenient——"

"Susan," began Mrs. Lyle, and started fiddling with her darning again.

Susan said, "Mummy, I don't think you need break it to me gently. I suppose you're going to send me off to boarding-school too?"

Mrs. Lyle must have been expecting a much more drastic reaction from Susan, because she looked extremely relieved and nodded. "Not till after Christmas, of course," she said, "and you don't mind really, do you? But you know that we always meant you to go to boarding-school seeing you were an only child, but somehow we drifted on. . . . However, this does seem a good time to change, because I do very badly want to go with Daddy on this trip and I feel I can leave you now that you're a bit older. And it will be nice for you at St. Ronan's with Midge and Charlotte——"

"Yes, but," said Susan, "am I not a bit too old altogether to be going to boarding-school for the first time? After all, I'll be fourteen in December——"

"Very elderly, I admit," said her mother, grinning at her, "but the headmistress seems to think that it will be all right. We'll get you fitted out before I go—it's going to be a rush. And you'll go up to London about the twenty-third of December—we sail the next day."

"Ugh," said Susan rather blankly, "*before* Christmas!"

"Yes, I'm sorry about that," said Mrs. Lyle, "but it wasn't possible to get a passage any later, for Daddy has to be in South Africa by the end of January. And you'll love being with your cousins for Christmas."

Susan suddenly felt rather abandoned and bleak. "Oh, yes, but they have the most terrifying parties," she said, with a horrible memory of extremely complicated pencil games at which she had conspicuously failed to shine.

"Oh, well, *parties*," said her mother. "They don't happen every day. It's not likely that they'd have more than one party each year, so you could face that, I should think."

Susan thought gloomily of battling her ignorant way through even one party, and sighed. "But of course," she said, brightening, "I might be ill in bed with a high temperature that day, mightn't I, and miss it?"

"Miss what?" said her mother, whose mind was now running on the vast numbers of new clothes that Susan would need, and of sewing name-tapes on them all.

"Miss the *party* of course," Susan was beginning, to her mother's bewilderment, when she was fortunately interrupted by a raucous and imperious mewing at the door.

Susan rose and opened the door and her Siamese cat stalked in. He began weaving himself round Susan's legs. "Oh, *Mummy*," cried Susan, dropping to her knees and scratching the cat in his favourite scratching places, "what about Chang?"

"It's all arranged," said Mrs. Lyle, snatching her mending and balls of wool out of Chang's reach. "Aunt Lucy says she'll be glad to have Chang too."

"But will Chang be glad to go?" said Susan.

"He'll be a very silly cat if he isn't," said Mrs. Lyle, "with that beautiful big garden to disport himself in."

"Yes, but it'll be rather a change for him," said Susan. "And for me too, of course——"

"Then you must console each other, if necessary," said her mother. "But you will be all right, won't you, darling?"

"Ugh, yes, of course," said Susan stoutly. "And it'll be fun for you going with Daddy for a change. Will you bring me back an elephant's tusk?"

Mrs. Lyle didn't know if elephants' tusks were easily come by, but promised to look out for one.

"Or those carvings of a lot of little elephants following each other," said Susan. "Those are nice. And you needn't worry about me, Mummy, I'll be fine."

"I'm sure you will," said her mother, fortunately unable to see into the future. "But, Susan," she added, a little anxiously, "you won't rescue anyone, will you?"

Susan blushed. All her life she had been befriending and even bringing home lame ducks, stray cats, lost dogs and even, not so long ago, a lost child who had turned out not to be lost after all, which had been very awkward for Susan. All had come right in the end fortunately, but Susan still felt hot with embarrassment at the very mention of the incident. "Of course not, Mother," she mumbled. As far as she was concerned, she felt, they could all rescue themselves, she wasn't going to lift a finger, and that went for animals *and* humans, but particularly humans, who simply misunderstood a girl all the time and talked about kidnappers. Animals at least didn't threaten to send you to prison, they only scratched or bit. Not that *that* was very nice, thought Susan, snatching her hand away from Chang, who was trying to gnaw it to the bone. Not that the ingratitude of humans or animals was now any concern of hers, because she was going to mind her own business henceforward. "I'll not be doing any more rescuing," she said emphatically.

"Oh, good," said Mrs. Lyle, and stopped looking anxious. They began to discuss the lists that Mrs. Lyle had had from St. Ronan's and how they were going to finish all the shopping in time, and Susan gave a sigh or two for all the friends she would leave behind her in her present school, but the glorious prospect of spending all her holidays in *London*, with the *Carmichaels*, soon banished all gloom.

CHAPTER TWO

TROUBLES

ALL the Carmichaels were on the platform at Euston to meet Susan. They gave her a rapturous welcome. Susan, as she always did on first meeting them again, felt a little shy of their effusiveness and what she indulgently called to herself their English ways, but if she didn't say very much, she was the only one who didn't.

Midge flung her arms round her and knocked her beret to a very rakish angle; Aunt Lucy came at her from one side and kissed her on both cheeks, Charlotte and Bill tried to get at her from the other but couldn't manage to elbow Uncle Charles out of the way, and had to content themselves with seizing her case and her waterproof and the basket containing Chang; it was with difficulty that she restrained them from snatching the coat off her back. All talking at once, they collected her luggage and bundled into the car which, being a new one, was a source of great pride to the family and had to be duly admired by Susan. Aunt Lucy and Bill went in front with Uncle Charles, and the girls went into the back. Midge took charge of Chang and opened his basket and made cooing noises over him while Susan, bouncing a little with excitement, craned her neck from side to side, catching glimpses of Aldwych and the Strand and Waterloo Bridge and exciting stretches of the Thames and the nice red London buses hurrying on their way.

The Carmichaels lived in Wichwood Village which, although, as Uncle Charles never tired of pointing out, was only five miles from St. Paul's, was really a village with little old shops and trim little cottages and Georgian houses, mellow and dignified. The village street was lined with trees, bare now in the chill December evening; it ran into Tollgate Road, where the Carmichaels' house stood, by the gates of Wichwood Park, the first of a group of gracious eighteenth-century houses. The two next door were joined together; the Carmichaels' stood by itself. Part of it was old too, but it had been added to in more recent years and was full of twists and corners and little unexpected flights of stairs. Susan thought that it was a most satisfactory house to live in—it had been wonderful for playing houses when she and Midge had been at that stage. They had all spent hours and days when they were little tapping and measuring and trying to find a secret passage—in fact it was doubtful if Susan had ever quite given up hope of at least a secret cupboard. Aunt Lucy had a desk with a secret drawer, which was always something, not of course that it was much of a secret by this time.

She was in the habit of keeping sixpences in it which she was trying to save up, but they never had a chance to come to anything as she was continually sending one of the family to her secret drawer for change.

Opposite the house was the Picture Gallery, which was quite famous, and in front of the houses in Tollgate Road were grass verges surrounded by black and white posts. There really was a toll-gate, too, farther up the road, a trap for unwary motorists who had to pay threepence or go round another way; and there was an old millpond where the Carmichael children had fed the ducks in their extreme youth. To Susan, coming from the tenements and drab greyness of Glasgow, Wichwood was like a fairy-tale village. To-night, as they came through, it looked cosy and gay. The little shops were bright and Christmassy; the toyshop had blobs of cotton-wool snow on its windows and crowds of little boys round its door.

In the windows of some of the houses Christmas trees gleamed and sparkled.

"We haven't decorated our tree yet," said Midge. "We waited till you came, Susan."

"Unfortunately," said Charlotte, "Bill sat on a box of decorations and ruined the lot—some of our best ones too, that we've had for *years*. But we're going to take him up to Harrod's to-morrow and make him buy some more. He says he hasn't got any money left after the expensive presents he has bought us all, but——"

"I can't *wait* to see the expensive presents," said Midge. "Railway lines and spare trucks if I know him——"

Bill leant over the back of the seat to deny this hotly, but they had arrived at the house and the argument was averted.

Bill insisted on taking Susan immediately to the back door to show her a little swinging panel that he had made in it for Chang, so that he could get in and out when he liked without the door being opened. Susan thought it was extremely clever and the neatest little gadget she had ever seen, and was sure that Chang would like it as much as she did, if not more. Bill beamed. Then Midge hurried Susan upstairs to the bedroom which they were to share, Charlotte having been promoted to a room of her own. It was a big room at the top of the house, looking to the front, with two little beds, two little wardrobes and two chests of drawers, all cream with garlands of flowers painted on them. The curtains and bedspreads were glazed chintz and the dressing-table had a glazed chintz frill. Susan was dumb with wonder.

Midge looked round with satisfaction. "It *is* nice, isn't it?" she said. "Aunt Lucy had it all done specially for us as a surprise. I nearly fainted when I came home from St. Ronan's yesterday.

Mind you, this room hadn't been painted for about a hundred years and it badly needed something, but it was very sweet of her to make it all so nice. That's the sickening bit—she *is* so sweet at times——"

Before Susan could ask for an explanation of this cryptic remark, the gong boomed and the girls hurried down to supper.

She got her explanation later.

After supper Uncle Charles went off to deal with a few belated patients, and Aunt Lucy sent the family up to the old schoolroom. "Off you go," she said, " there's a nice fire up there, and Miss Pershore is coming in to let me hear some new gramophone records, so we shall want peace in the drawing-room. But it's early to bed to-night, remember, Susan has had a tiring day. Oh, yes, Bill, you may stay up for a little."

The old schoolroom was on the top floor too but in the old part of the house; it was low in the ceiling and panelled and a little flight of stairs led down to it, and when the fire was lit it looked like a cosy little cave, or so Susan thought as she went down the steps. There were low bookshelves round the walls, crowded with the family's books, from the Beatrix Potters and *Little Grey Rabbit* books of their nursery days to Bill's present taste in railway manuals. There was a big battered table, which seemed to thrive on the ink, paint and cocoa which had been spilt on it from time to time; the chairs were old, the springs broken in the right places, and delightfully comfortable. Chang stretched himself out in front of the bright log fire, purring like a small and rather rusty engine: Susan lay prone in one of the broken-springed chairs; Charlotte fished some chocolate out of her desk and passed it round.

"Nut-milk," said Susan. "My favourite sort ——" She sighed blissfully. "And to-morrow is Christmas Eve, and—ugh, it's going to be fun!"

"Yes," said Midge, "if only——" and she sighed too, but not blissfully, "if only we weren't in such terrible trouble."

Susan sat up so quickly that a piece of nut went down the wrong way. She choked and coughed till the tears streamed, and Midge and Charlotte thumped her on the back and Bill offered her some water in a jam-jar which had obviously had poster paint in it very recently. Chang leapt out of the way with a reproachful look in his bright blue eyes.

Susan gradually coughed herself back to normal. "In terrible trouble!" she gasped, her head filled with visions of Uncle Charles ruined and the family lined up for the nearest workhouse. "Is Uncle Charles——?"

"It's not Daddy. He only laughs," said Midge gloomily. "It's Aunt Lucy."

"But—but Aunt Lucy seems all right," said Susan. "In fact," she added, remembering how merry everyone had been at supper, "you all seem quite bright."

"Oh," said Midge, "we're putting a brave face on it, but she's ruining our lives."

"Yes," agreed Charlotte, "she has always had dotty ideas but she has never actually ruined our lives before."

Midge, to Susan's surprise but also relief, suddenly giggled. "Oh, Charlotte," she said, "will you *ever* forget the time she had the craze for hand-loom weaving?" Charlotte began to giggle too. "She wove those revolting pieces of sack-cloth," Midge explained to Susan, "rough and *hairy*, I can't tell you how awful they were, and had them made up into dresses for us. Mine was grey and Charlotte's was sort of porridge-coloured, and she made us wear them——"

"And they were so tickly," said Charlotte, "we scratched madly all day long, until Midge came out in a horrid rash."

"I have a *very* sensitive skin," said Midge smugly.

"And poor Aunt Lucy had to cut them up for floor-cloths. Wonderful floor-cloths they were too, they *never* wore out."

"You can imagine how they would have worn as dresses," said Midge. "We should have been in them still but for my sensitive skin."

"And then the time," Charlotte went on, "when she made us all go vegetarian. We ate nut cutlets till even the squirrels in Howlet's Green gave us very sour looks."

"And we'd *still* have been on a diet of dandelion leaves or whatever," said Midge, "if I hadn't come out *again* in a rash——"

"Was that your sensitive skin too?" said Susan.

"No, it was measles, as a matter of fact," said Midge, "but Aunt Lucy didn't tumble to that until she'd given all the dandelion leaves to the rabbits and burnt her nut recipe books."

"But," said Bill, looking up from a very complicated meccano model with which he was busy in a corner, "d'you remember the time she read a book by some wizard schoolmaster or other who said that children must be allowed to do exactly what they liked or terrible things would happen to their characters? That was smashing!"

"Smashing is the right word," said Charlotte. "Bill was at a very experimental stage in his life, and Aunt Lucy gave him a vicious-looking clasp-knife he had a fancy for, and he'd smashed the gramophone and carved up an old clock and was just starting in on the piano when Daddy intervened and said he'd take a chance on our future characters but he certainly wouldn't have us in the house if we were going to go about with knives in our teeth and breaking up the piano."

"Yes, Bill rather overdid the whole business," said Midge. "But it was one of Aunt Lucy's better ideas, I must say."

"But what idea has Aunt Lucy got this time?" said Susan, who had known, of course, that Aunt Lucy was inclined to be a bit potty at times, but had no idea that it had gone to such lengths.

"Well," said Charlotte slowly, "it's a little difficult to put it in one word, but the general idea is that we must go in for culture in a big way. She has always encouraged us to like books and pictures and music, of course, and that was all right, but she has gone quite hopelessly highbrow. For instance she wants to get rid of all our nice old pictures and hang up the most awful things."

"The one she offered me," said Bill in a voice of gloom, "had a dead fish growing out of a lady's hat. I told her I didn't care for it, and if she didn't like my present collection which I've had for *years* I'd hang up a Hornby train catalogue instead."

"And what a to-do there was over our Christmas cards," said Midge. "She whisked away all the ones which we had bought with robins and snow and bits of holly on them, and gave us some reproductions of very modern pictures to send."

"To be perfectly honest," said Charlotte, "some of them were nice, but I do like a little bit of holly at Christmas-time."

Susan was amazed. "But doesn't Aunt Lucy *like* holly and snow and robins?" she asked.

"Seemingly not," said Midge. "But anyway, I sneaked all our nice Christmassy ones back again and we sent them just the same. The girls at school would have had nightmares if they'd got some of the things Aunt Lucy expected us to send. There was one of a clown who looked as if he had been dead for years."

"And," Bill went on with his list of Aunt Lucy's iniquities, "she has booked seats for *Cinderella* for Boxing Day."

"Ugh, but that will be great," said Susan, who had no doubts this time. "*Cinderella* is my favourite pantomime."

"It's not a pantomime," said Bill scornfully, "it's a *bally*."

"We don't really agree with Bill about this," said Midge, "because Charlotte and I are quite keen on ballet. We've told him he'll like it when he sees it."

"Oh, me too!" said Susan, who wasn't difficult to please. "I'll like seeing anything, really."

Bill snorted and went back to his meccano.

Susan said, thinking over what they had been saying, "The only thing is, I can't quite make out how you could call that ruining your lives."

"Oh," cried Charlotte, "there's more to it than that. That's only the general set-up. I want to be a nurse and she won't let me. Oh, no! Just because I can draw a little I've got to go to the Slade or somewhere and become an artist."

"And I," said Midge, "am to leave St. Ronan's and go to some ghastly school where they do nothing but ballet so that I can be a ballerina."

"Oh, *no*!" said Susan, "not just when I'm going to St. Ronan's! Besides," she added, "*I* didn't know that you were a good dancer, Midge."

Midge glided out of her chair and did an *arabesque* in a corner.

Susan was suitably impressed.

"Oh, do sit down, Midge," said Charlotte, without turning her head.

"Sit *down*, Midge," said Bill, "you nearly put your great hoof on my crane then."

Midge pirouetted across the room and sank gracefully and affectedly into her chair again.

"As a matter of fact," said Charlotte, "although you wouldn't think so, she's not bad."

"But it would be great to go to a school where you did nothing but dance all day," said Susan, her eyes gleaming at the thought of all the arithmetic, French and science you couldn't do if you were dancing.

"Well, my love," said Midge, "let Aunt Lucy send *you* to this dancing school."

Susan giggled. "Have you ever seen me dance?" she said. "But, Midge, wouldn't you like it?"

"I should loathe it," said Midge. "My knees

would knock so much I'd be put in the orchestra among the castanets, if they have castanets in an orchestra. And do you know," she said, sitting up and pointing a solemn finger at Susan, "do you know that you have to practise for *hours* every day? Not minutes, *hours*. And do you know, that even when you're a *prima ballerina* you can't relax and put your feet up, you *still* have to practise for *hours* every day? Honestly, I'd die. Quite seriously, my health wouldn't stand it. But Aunt Lucy won't believe me."

"Nobody could believe that laziness like yours could exist," said Charlotte. "But even so I still don't see why you should be a dancer if you don't want to be a dancer."

"Usually it's the other way," commented Susan. "Girls want to be dancers and their aunts won't let them."

"Either way it's not the thing," said Charlotte. "It's *our* career, after all. Why shouldn't I be a nurse if I want to?"

"But, Charlotte," said Susan, "you can't start being a nurse when you're only sixteen. Aunt Lucy may have another idea by the time you're old enough to go to a hospital and train."

"Yes, I know," agreed Charlotte. "But the point is that I've got to decide now which subjects I'll take in my General Certificate, and naturally I want to take subjects which would be useful in nursing and drop Latin, and Aunt Lucy won't let me. If my drawing isn't good enough to go in for art, she says, then I must go to a university, and of course I need Latin for that. Or so she says."

"If only Aunt Lucy didn't want us to be clever and interesting and have interesting careers," sighed Midge, "like families in books."

"But I think you *are* clever and interesting," said Susan.

"Oh, *do* you?" said Midge, looking pleased.

"Well—interesting," said Susan.

"Oh!" said Midge.

From his corner among the meccano Bill suddenly said, "Aunt Lucy was all right until she got so friendly with the Plum. Jolly sporting she was," he added sadly.

"Oh, that's true," said Charlotte. "The Plum's the nigger in the woodpile, all right."

Susan thought that she must be even more stupid than she already suspected. "The *plum?*" she said.

"Of course, Susan hasn't met the Plum yet," said Midge. "You will, my dear, you will. She's coming to us for Christmas dinner, and we're going to a party at her house in the evening."

Susan hadn't expected her social life to include going to parties with a plum. She looked vacantly from Midge to Charlotte.

Charlotte laughed at her and began to explain. "The Plum," she said, "is Miss Pershore, who lives at Number Fourteen. Number Twelve, next door, is empty you know; at least it's full of furniture because Ivor Williams the furniture people have it as a store—isn't it a shame that a lovely old house like that should be used as a furniture store? But anyway, Miss Pershore came to live at Number Fourteen just over a year ago, and she and Aunt Lucy are as thick as thieves."

"She calls her 'Loocher,'" interrupted Bill gloomily.

"*Loocher?*" said Susan.

"'Lucia,'" said Charlotte impatiently. "It's Italian or something for Lucy. And they're fearfully highbrow. Go to exhibitions of terrible pictures and listen to Third Programme sort of music together for hours——"

"They're at it now, in the drawing-room," said Midge. "You can't think what some of the Plum's records are like."

"Rather like some of the noises Chang makes, as a matter of fact," said Bill.

"Oh, help," said Susan.

"Yes, well, the Plum's mad on that kind of music and highbrow plays and stuff. Although I must say she's also mad on puppets—marionettes, you know—and they're great fun. She makes them herself, and she has a wonderful little stage—do you know anything about puppets? They've been going for hundreds of years, and all over Europe—Miss Plum lent me a book about them. She'll probably give us a show on Christmas Day. She gives shows all over the place—she goes to Paris nearly every week, only I think that's more just for culture. She has been helping to organise an exhibition on the theatre too, in town. She's showing some of her puppets in the toy theatre and puppet section and she has promised to take us to see it. If only," said Charlotte, "she'd stick to the puppets and let us choose our own careers. She has led poor Aunt Lucy completely astray."

"Yes," said Midge, "*she* told Aunt Lucy about this awful ballet school."

"And *she* thinks that I should foster my artistic gift as she calls it," said Charlotte, "but she's wrong if she thinks I'm going to paint dead clowns and fish growing out of hats. But I shouldn't mind drawing—well, animals, like Chang for instance, or illustrating children's books in my spare time between taking temperatures."

"I always understood that nurses didn't have any spare time," said Midge.

"Oh, I don't expect Aunt Lucy is serious about all this," said Susan. "She'll get over it."

"Well, it won't be much use her getting over it if I've been moved to this school in the meantime," said Midge.

"Or if I miss my chance of concentrating on

subjects which will be of some use to me," said Charlotte.

Susan agreed gloomily. She went on, "And what about Bill? Is she ruining his life too?"

"Oh, well, Bill hasn't a hope of getting what he wants, thank goodness," said Charlotte, "because he keeps nagging at Aunt Lucy to move to Limehouse or some squalid part of the Old Kent Road where crime is rampant——"

"What?" said Susan.

"*Bill* isn't taking to crime," said Midge soothingly, "it's on account of his friend Joe's promotion."

Susan looked interested, but bewildered.

"Joe is Joe Taylor," explained Charlotte, "his mother is Mrs. Taylor who is our help and who is a perfect darling and has been with us for ages and ages, and Joe's a policeman and——"

"And Joe's mad to get into the C.I.D.," interrupted Bill, "that's the Criminal Investigation Department," he explained kindly, "but he'll never get noticed for the C.I.D. unless he has some interesting cases to deal with—you know, murders."

"Oh, help!" said Susan.

"Well, it needn't be murders," said Bill impatiently, "big jewel robberies would do or gangs of black marketeers, but what chance has he in a place like Wichwood where *nothing* of that kind *ever* happens? Now if we lived in a really exciting neighbourhood I could put Joe on to all sorts of things and he'd get promoted in no time."

"It seems to me," said Susan diffidently, "that it would be simpler for *Joe* to go and live in a more exciting neighbourhood."

"That's what I say," said Charlotte, "but actually Joe can't because of Mrs. Taylor who lives in the dearest little house in Millpond Cottages—you know, up Tollgate Road, looking on to the pond—and Joe lives with her."

"Yes," said Bill bitterly, "and all he gets to do is chase boys for throwing sticks at the chestnut trees in the conker season."

"Oh, conkers do you call them?" said Susan with interest. "We call them chessies——"

At that point Aunt Lucy appeared, looking for Bill to chase *him* off to bed.

Bill started what he considered an irrefutable argument for staying up a little later, but Aunt Lucy was adamant. "And in half an hour, Midge," she said, "I'll be after you and Susan. Look at the poor lamb, she can hardly keep her eyes open."

"Ugh, Aunt Lucy, I'm not at all sleepy," protested Susan.

"Well, all right—half an hour," said Aunt Lucy and dragged Bill off.

"Poor old Bill," said Midge, "he's longing to do something for Joe. He cuts interesting pieces out of the papers and gives them to Joe to tantalise him. But he still nags at Aunt Lucy, the chump."

"I can't blame Aunt Lucy for holding out about that," said Susan. "You could hardly call that ruining his life."

"No, but alas," said Charlotte, "I'm afraid the poor old chap's life is going to be ruined on Christmas morning, because he has set his heart on getting an electric train, but it's all Lombard Street to a china orange that he's not going to get it."

"Miss Plum again?" said Susan.

"Well, I don't know about that," said Charlotte. "Aunt Lucy hasn't told us what Bill is getting but I'm sure Miss Plum wouldn't be enthusiastic about electric trains. No, the thing is, they cost the *earth*. I think that will be the reason rather than Miss Plum's highbrow tastes."

Midge said, "Bother Miss Plum. It's not as if we didn't like the things that Miss Plum and Aunt Lucy think we should like—we do—apart from dead clowns, I mean—but we like other things as well. We love ballet, but I don't want to *be* a ballet dancer. And Miss Plum makes such a *fuss* always—I sometimes think that she's not a genuine lover of the arts at all—that she puts it on."

"Why can't Miss Plum mind her own business?" said Susan. "And anyway, why d'you call her Miss Plum?"

"You're ignorant," said Midge, "as you would

say yourself. Pershore is a famous place for plums."

"Su-u-u-san! Mi-i-idge!" called Aunt Lucy.

Later Susan sat up in her delightful little painted bed, hugging her knees.

"Midge," she said, "can't we do something to help Charlotte?"

Midge was brushing her hair, rather half-heartedly. "What do you suggest?" she said.

"Ugh, I don't know," said Susan. "Supposing —supposing Aunt Lucy became dangerously ill and Charlotte nursed her back to life and Aunt Lucy was terribly grateful and let her be a nurse?"

"Aunt Lucy's never ill," said Midge.

"Yes but," said Susan, "couldn't she *be* ill? Couldn't we push her out into the snow or something and *make* her ill?"

"It would need to be ' something,'" said Midge, "because there's no snow."

"But I'm sure it's going to snow," said Susan. "The sky looked very louring and grey to-day and there was snow on Shap when we came over it. I thought that maybe the train would stick in a snowdrift and we'd be snowed up, but it didn't."

"I can't think how we'd get poor Aunt Lucy to Shap," said Midge. "Besides, I don't think that you need worry about Charlotte too much.

You should know by this time that she's rather like Aunt Lucy herself—gets ideas. Last year she wanted to be a Wren because she was friendly with Tibby Weston whose father is in the Navy; and then this term she got very pally with Daphne Terry. It won't surprise you to learn that Daphne's going in for nursing. Besides, she's *always* thinking up some reason for dropping Latin."

Susan may or may not have been listening to Midge. She said obstinately, "I don't see why Charlotte shouldn't be a nurse if she wants to. It's a noble career."

Midge grinned. "We none of us consider that Charlotte is suited to be a nurse." She jumped into bed, and then jumped out again to put off the gas-fire and open the curtains. "I believe it's freezing, if that's any help to you," she said, looking out. In Tollgate Road there was a sparkle about the trees and grass verges in the light of the street lamps.

But Susan lay thinking and planning and wondering how she could rescue Charlotte from the tyranny of Aunt Lucy. . . . As for Charlotte not making a good nurse, she thought, she was sure that that was utter nonsense. . . . And she would look so pretty in those white caps . . . so pretty. . . .

"Good-night," said Midge, climbing back into bed.

But Susan was already asleep.

CHAPTER THREE

A HINT UNHEEDED

THERE was a bright sparkle in the air next morning; and a bright sparkle about Susan too. She was so excited that· she woke long before Bill came thumping on their door, and was up and dressed before Midge—that notorious late-riser—had thought of dragging herself out of bed.

"Midge," she called over to the huddle in the bed, "aren't you *ever* going to get up?"

"M-m-mm," growled Midge.

Susan set to work on her, and by leaving out teeth and bath, indeed any washing at all, managed to get her down to breakfast when the gong sounded. That this was quite a feat was made clear by the exclamations of the other members of the family and Aunt Lucy said that Susan must be a good influence on Midge. Midge said loftily that she couldn't understand what all the fuss was about, and anyway, they wanted to get away early, didn't they, if they were going up to town to show Susan the sights?

"Oh, not *sights*," said Susan, "shops."

"Shops, of course, on Christmas Eve," said Aunt Lucy. "Would you like to have lunch in town? Because I could come up later and meet you if you like, but I'd have to be back early to get all the odds and ends in for Christmas."

The girls thought that lunch in town would be a wonderful idea, and Bill agreed, so long as it wasn't one of those dainty lunches; and they arranged that the girls and Bill should take Susan in buses up Regent Street, along Oxford Street, then down Park Lane and along Knightsbridge to Harrod's. These were all thrilling names to Susan, and she beamed her delight at this arrangement. Aunt Lucy interrupted poor Uncle Charles at his *Times* and bullied him into letting her have the car for an hour or two, and arranged to meet the party in the marble hall at Harrod's, which sounded very grand to Susan.

"Susan," said Bill, probably sensing in her a fellow-spirit, "have you seen this bit in the paper?"

"How could Susan see anything in the paper when you've been hanging on to it like a limpet?" said Midge.

Bill gave Midge a quelling look and pointed out the passage to Susan. Susan read:

TWO WATCH-SMUGGLERS ARE FINED £16,000

From Our Own Correspondent

DOVER, Wednesday.

Two men—one from Paris, the other from London—were each fined £8,000 or 12 months' jail here to-day for trying to smuggle watches.

The man from Paris, Jules Renard, brought 612 watches, worth £7,073, hidden in a secret compartment in his car.

The man from London, Frederick Benson, brought in 922 watches, worth £24,657—330 of them in a belt round his body, the others in the false bottoms of two cases.

The judge gave it as his opinion that there must be a gang of these watch-smugglers at work, so often did men and women charged with attempted evasion of Customs duties appear in the courts.

Then she said, "Yes, it's very interesting, but I don't see how it's going to help Joe."

"I know," said Bill, "stuck here in a quiet law-abiding suburb like Wichwood. He'd like to catch a gang—like this smuggling gang in the paper."

Susan's eyes gleamed. Then she took a bite of toast as her thoughts ranged rather sadly over Wichwood—so quiet, so gracious and beautiful. It certainly didn't suggest itself as a hide-out for gangsters, she thought. "But after all," she said to Bill, "the *head* of the gang has got to live *somewhere*. Although I must say it doesn't seem likely that it would be in Wichwood."

"Joe keeps on hoping," said Bill. "He'll be interested in this smuggling. He can go snooping

round cars for false compartments. And I'll
help him when I have time——"

Susan thought that she would quite like to
help too. Bill seemed doubtful whether it was
a job for a girl, but before he could make any
definite pronouncements, Charlotte wanted to
know if Susan and Bill were going to be at the
breakfast-table all morning.

"I've finished," said Bill. "Aunt Lucy, will you
please keep this *Daily Mail* for me and not let
anyone tear it up?"

"Well, Bill," said Aunt Lucy, "you know that
Mrs. Taylor will use it to light a fire as soon as
she gets her hands on it, so you'd better put it in
some safe place— but not before I've seen it. Yes,
all right, I'll hide it for you."

"Come *on*, Bill," said Midge, "or Susan won't
have time to see any shops before lunch."

Regent Street was gay with Christmas trees.
Susan said she just couldn't believe that she was
really in a street that she had read about in books
so often, and Bill said that seeing they were in
Regent Street, she ought to visit Hamley's, which
was a very famous shop. So they all got off the
bus and good-naturedly went with Bill to Hamley's to gaze at the electric trains which were
whizzing round in a most realistic manner, even
to having smoke puffing out of the little engines.
They only got him away, indeed, by promising

him more trains at Harrod's. Once at Harrod's, poor Bill was torn between the toy trains and the escalators and travelled twice up to the top floor and down again trying to make up his mind where to spend his time. This naturally became rather boring for the girls, waiting for him at the bottom of the moving staircases.

"We can't wait here all day," said Charlotte impatiently. Susan, who found the escalators fascinating too, said in her helpful way that she would go and find him, and that was the last that Charlotte and Midge saw of either of them for some time, except for occasional glimpses of them going up when the girls were going down, or going down when the girls were soaring up. They eventually made up on Susan, however, who was helping a small boy to get off at the first floor. The small boy didn't want her help: in fact if anyone needed help it was Susan. Charlotte and Midge came on them as they landed in a heap on the floor together, the small boy insisting that he hadn't fallen, he'd been *pushed*, and Susan vainly trying to rescue her hat, which was her best one, from the small boy's feet. Bill at this point arrived too, having decided on the trains, but when he saw Susan, hatless in the middle of the mêlée, he walked quickly away, pretending not to know her. Giggling helplessly, the three girls eventually followed him to the Toy Fair.

Susan had never in her life seen such a wonderful array of all conceivable kinds of toys; the whole vast display done up in imitation of a fair, with Father Christmas in a caravan. She could do nothing but gaze and gape, and had to be dragged off by Charlotte and Midge to help choose some Christmas tree decorations.

"Bill's supposed to pay for these," Midge grumbled.

"If you like to try to get him away from the trains you're welcome," said Charlotte. "*I* think it would be quicker to buy them ourselves."

"All right," said Midge, "let's get a lovely lot and make Bill pay for them. Let's have those, and those—and a box of those!"

"Only a millionaire could pay for that lot," said Charlotte, after a shuddering glance at the prices. However they eventually decided on one or two bright shining balls, and plenty of tinsel, because that seemed to be a lot of glitter for the money; and Susan bought a packet of silver stuff in strands which she knew made most effective icicles when hung over the dark branches.

They met Aunt Lucy in the "marble hall" which, after all, to Susan's disappointment, was only a sort of bank and probably not marble at all, although there were a nice lot of comfortable chairs for people to sit on while waiting. Lunch was a great success, not at all dainty, and Aunt Lucy let them have what they liked and not what she thought would be good for them, and they had lots of fizzy lemonade and finished up with ice-cream.

When they reached home, there were piles of exciting-looking parcels to be prodded and rattled before Aunt Lucy bore them all away until the next day; and lots of Christmas cards which they arranged on the drawing-room mantelshelf. Then they brought in the tree, which had been keeping fresh in the garden, and Midge and Charlotte began to decorate it.

"Oh, I'll help," cried Susan, and in the next ten minutes had knocked the tree over twice through a misunderstanding of what Charlotte wanted done with it. What with Susan helping and Bill asking weren't they nearly ready *yet* for him to arrange the fairy-lights, Midge and Charlotte were nearly distracted, when Aunt Lucy came in and asked Bill to deliver to an old lady a pot of hyacinths which had been overlooked in the general bustle. Susan offered to take it, but as it was extremely unlikely that she would ever find her way, Charlotte suggested that Susan and Bill might go together.

It was when they were coming back down Tollgate Road and the darkness was beginning to fall that Susan noticed a car standing outside one of the houses.

"There's a car," she said.

"So what?" said Bill.

"We could examine that one for false compart-ments," said Susan.

"Oh, no we couldn't," said Bill. "That one belongs to Major Banks."

"So what?" said Susan in her turn.

"Major Banks is an ogre," said Bill in a fearful whisper. "He *eats* little children."

Susan jumped: then she laughed a little shame-facedly. "Ugh, away, you daft scone," she said.

"When we were kids," said Bill, "we really believed he did: even now I shouldn't put it past him. I'm not searching his car."

Susan said, "And I thought you were anxious about Joe's promotion?"

"I am," Bill said, "and it's all very well for you to talk, but you don't know Major Banks."

"Well, one of us can keep watch while the other searches the car," said Susan. "We would never get anywhere unless we took an occasional risk."

Bill couldn't help feeling that he'd rather the occasional risk didn't involve Major Banks, but he wasn't going to have a mere girl outdoing him in nerve. He looked up and down Tollgate Road. It was almost dark by now, and there were lights in Major Banks' house; but not a soul was in sight. "All right," he said. "I'll search and you keep guard."

They crossed the road, and the grass verge, to where the car was standing. "Perhaps it's locked," said Bill hopefully. But it wasn't. The car was an Armstrong-Siddeley of great age, but beautifully kept. Bill reluctantly opened one of the rear doors. "How d'you imagine you look for secret compartments?" he said.

"Really, I suppose," said Susan, practically breathing down his neck in her eagerness, "we should have a knife and do a bit of slashing."

"Oh, glory," said Bill, visualising Major Banks' reactions to finding the leather-work of his car all slashed. "Do keep your eyes open, Susan," he said.

"I am," said Susan, casting a casual glance at the silent house, and then quickly turning her attention again to Bill. Bill was cautiously and rather half-heartedly feeling the pockets on the doors and underneath the windows. "What about the floor-boards," said Susan, "couldn't we prise them up?"

"We certainly couldn't," said Bill. "Hallo, what's this?" he said, with his hand down the back of the seat.

"What? What?" said Susan, pushing her head inside the car too, and hopping from one foot to another in her excitement.

"Oh, nothing!" said Bill, letting the light from the street lamp shine on his find. "Only an old A.A. Handbook."

At that moment there was a sort of bellowing roar behind them. Bill gave such a start backwards that he knocked into Susan, who straightened up and cracked her head on the top of the doorway. Feeling slightly stunned, she looked up and had one terrifying glimpse of an immensely tall man coming across the road towards them and shaking his fist—or it might be a club or a gun—at them.

"What do you young scoundrels think you're doing?" shouted this fearful apparition.

"Run! Run!" yelled Bill. He slammed shut the car door and took to his heels up Tollgate Road. Susan went after him. "Over this gate, quick," panted Bill. Susan half-fell over the gate and stumbled after the dim figure of Bill across what seemed like a ploughed field interspersed with occasional barbed-wire fences and tank traps. Behind them came the infuriated roars of Major Banks.

"Ugh, Bill, where *are* we?" said Susan, when she felt that she could stumble and struggle no longer.

"Actually, these are allotments," said Bill. "There used to be a couple of houses here with big gardens, but they're allotments now."

"Oh, help!" said Susan. "I suppose those were brussel sprout stalks I was knocking into. I thought they were tank traps. Can't we go back to the road, Bill?"

"And face Major Banks?" said Bill.

"Oh, *help!*" said Susan. "Why did you come

this way at all?" she said. "Why didn't you run for home? We would have been there by now."

"And Major Banks would have been there too, thundering on the door and demanding our heads from Daddy. And Daddy and he are at daggers drawn already because this sort of thing used to crop up occasionally when we were kids. No, no, we were safer coming this way. We can get through to the park from here, I should think."

"But the park gates will be closed by now. I heard the whistle ages ago," said Susan, with a vision of the two of them spending Christmas Eve in the park.

"I know," said Bill, "but I know a way into our own garden from the park. At least I do in daylight—oh, good, through this broken fence, Susan—if we break it a little bit more—we're in the park. *Now* we're all right."

Susan was glad he thought so, but as it was thanks to her that they were in their present predicament she said nothing, but ploughed after him, across really very difficult terrain, in a sort of shrubbery where it was pitch dark, and where there were countless holes and tree-stumps to fall over. "Why don't I mind my own business," she grumbled, "and let Joe look after his own promotion?"

"Why don't you keep guard, when you're supposed to keep guard?" said Bill.

"Well, I didn't expect him to come *that* way,"

said Susan. "I was watching the house. More or less."

"Well, watch your feet, more or less, now," Bill advised her, "for there's a little stream about here."

"Oh, help!" said Susan. However, without mishap they came to the gap in the fence between the park and the Carmichaels' garden which Bill knew of, and found themselves in the small orchard which lay at the bottom of their garden. They crossed the orchard and were thankful to come to the little lane which ran between their house and the park, separating the garden proper and the orchard, and leading, oddly enough, to Miss Pershore's garage. Miss Pershore's car was standing outside it.

"There's a car," said Susan, all their recent troubles forgotten.

"This is where we came in," said Bill. "Fortunately, this is Miss Plum's car, so we needn't examine *it*."

Susan was walking round the beautiful Rolls Royce saloon. "It would be interesting to have a look round it just to get an idea where there *might* be secret compartments," said Susan.

"We could do that with Daddy's car," said Bill.

"Yes, but," said Susan, "will we ever get the chance? He's always in it."

"It's too dark," said Bill.

"Bill," said Susan, ignoring this, "you're mechanically minded. If you wanted to have a secret compartment in your car, where would you have it?"

Bill considered a little and then said, "Well, I don't know where *I* would have it, but I once read a story where it was in the petrol tank."

"In the petrol tank!" shrieked Susan. "You couldn't put smuggled watches in among the petrol!"

"Naturally not," said Bill patiently. "The tank would only hold, say, two gallons of petrol; the rest of the space would be taken up with the secret compartment."

Susan hunted about on the ground and eventually, in spite of the darkness, found a stick.

"Here's a stick," she said in her helpful way. "Measure the petrol space in Miss Plum's tank now."

"Really, Susan!" said Bill in an affronted voice. "You're not suggesting that Miss Plum smuggles in her spare time!"

"Ugh, well, I haven't met her, so I wouldn't know," said Susan cheerfully.

"She's a friend of Aunt Lucy's," said Bill stiffly.

Susan had the grace to feel slightly abashed. "Ugh, I'm sorry, Bill," she said. "I'm blethering. Let's go home."

At practically the same moment Bill realised that he was being rather touchy about nothing, and began to giggle. "Wait till you *do* meet her!" he said. "Anything less like a shady smuggler!"

Susan said, "Yes, it would be just a bit too much to expect to find something peculiar at our very first shot."

"Second shot," said Bill, with a shuddering memory of Major Banks.

"Come on, then," said Susan, "I'm getting cold, and Midge and Charlotte will be wondering where we've got to."

"It's a bit late to start worrying about that," said Bill.

They ran through the garden, and in by the back door, and rushed into the warmth and brightness of the drawing-room.

"Where on earth have you been?" demanded Charlotte. "Tea's ready and you haven't put the lights on the tree."

"Oh, the tree!" gasped Susan. "It's lovely!" She was allowed to drape her icicles on it, and Bill brought out his precious fairy-lights and arranged them in the branches and actually made them work, which impressed Susan very much. They seemed to impress Chang too. He came into the drawing-room to see what was going on and had Bill in a frenzy when he began to pat one of the lights softly with his cocoa-brown paws.

"Take Chang away!" Bill begged. "If one of those lights goes, they all go——"

"How peculiar," said Susan. "Come along, Chang, my wee precious, you come and play with your little swing-door—he's quite getting the idea about the door, Bill—and I'll give you a little ball of tinsel for your very own."

In the middle of tea Charlotte suddenly said, "Good gracious, I quite forgot to tell Susan about the carols. Susan, can you sing?"

"Well——" said Susan.

"Yes, well never mind," said Charlotte, "if you can't then you must just open your mouth without any sound coming out—you know, like a goldfish."

"Sing *The Holly and the Ivy*, and we'll see," commanded Midge.

"What, *now*?" said Susan, taking a piece of cake away from her mouth.

"Oh, let Susan finish her tea," said Aunt Lucy.

Midge explained that she and Charlotte and Bill and some girls went round their friends' houses carol-singing on Christmas Eve. "It's great fun, and we take a collection and send it to one of Aunt Lucy's pet charities," she said.

"I could always go round with the collecting-box," Susan said, "if you won't let me sing."

"Well, Bill does that, I'm afraid," said Midge. "He insists that all the old ladies are so touched by his bea-u-tiful voice that they put in an extra shilling. Actually, of course, they're in such a hurry to get rid of him that it's cheap at the price."

"Nothing of the kind," said Bill loftily. "You know quite well that Mrs. Evans is always in tears when I sing the solo bit in *We Three Kings of Orient Are*."

"Yes, well, Bill, old boy," said Midge, patting him gently on the shoulder, "don't let's go into why Mrs. Evans is in tears."

"Shall I sing now?" said Susan diplomatically.

"Yes, do, darling," said Aunt Lucy, rather absently, "that would be very nice."

"*The Holly and the Ivy*," sang Susan quaveringly, "*when they are both full-grown*."

"Okay, okay," interrupted her judges. "It might not get you to the Albert Hall, but you're in tune. You may sing." Susan was suitably and humbly grateful.

"Come on," said Charlotte, "it's time we were going——"

Susan thought that she would never forget that first time she went carol-singing. In the cold frosty evening they tramped happily from house to house; stars glittered in the sky, Christmas trees glittered in the windows as they passed; the lamps hanging outside the pretty doorways shone on their young, serious faces as they sang; Bill's treble, piercingly sweet, rang out in the solo parts. And it was quite true, Mrs. Evans *was* rather dewy-eyed, and put five shillings in the box.

It was when the carol-singers were working

their way along the big, gracious houses in Wichwood Common that Susan first noticed the policeman following them. At first, naturally, she thought nothing of it, but as they went from house to house and the policeman went too, she began to get so nervous that it did things to her singing, and made Bill glance at her once or twice. Eventually, when they were crossing the road by the old millpond on their way to Millpond Cottages, she whispered to Midge, "Midge, is carol-singing against the law or something? Can we be put in prison for it?"

"I dare say some people would *like* to put us in prison for it," said Midge, "but I don't think that they actually *could*——"

"Well, there's been a policeman following us for ages," said Susan.

"Oh, goodness, that's not a policeman, that's Joe," said Midge, "if you know what I mean. He always follows us round on Christmas Eve if he happens to be on duty. He seems to like the carols."

Well, this was certainly a relief to Susan, and without further incident, at half-past eight or so, when they had gone the round of their friends, they finished up at the Carmichaels' house, and then all trooped in for hot sausage rolls and cocoa and toasted sandwiches which Aunt Lucy had waiting for them at the drawing-room fire.

Uncle Charles had taken time off from his

patients to put sprigs of holly behind the pictures.
Aunt Lucy, who loved the festive time, had log
fires roaring in the hall, the drawing-room and
the schoolroom; from the kitchen came delicious
wafts from the turkey giblets simmering in
preparation for the next day. And then Aunt
Lucy bustled Bill off to bed, and suggested that
the girls should go pretty soon too, although they
could first come and help her in the kitchen to
prepare vegetables for the Christmas dinner.
Midge said she was sorry, *she* couldn't help, for
having missed her bath in the morning she would
have to have one now; so Aunt Lucy told her
that she must superintend Bill's bath first then,
and make sure that he remembered his ears and
all the other bits he was apt to overlook. Charlotte and Susan peeled piles of potatoes and prepared mounds of sprouts, and took the brown
skins off the chestnuts, which was a rather nicer
job than you would think, because you could
enjoy a frequent nibble at the chestnuts. Aunt
Lucy stuffed the turkey, and then there was a
minor crisis because they couldn't get it back
into the refrigerator, and where were they going
to put it out of Chang's reach? Chang, actually,
had been slinking round their legs and crying
piteously for some time, so Aunt Lucy chopped
up the giblets for him, and when he was thus
diverted they hid the turkey in the oven.

When Charlotte and Susan went upstairs, they

were disgusted to find Midge with her feet up by the schoolroom fire reading a book.

"And we've been downstairs working our fingers to the bone," said Charlotte.

"I don't think you should speak to me in that cross voice on Christmas Eve," said Midge. "After all, it's the season of peace and goodwill. And I've hung up your stockings for you—come and see!"

The other two did feel that that was one job they could quite well have managed for themselves, but everything was so exciting and nice and Christmasy that it certainly wasn't worth while having words with Midge. Bill was asleep in his little room, but he opened one eye and wanted to know if it was time for stockings. Charlotte told him not to be daft, they hadn't gone to bed yet, and Bill said that he simply *couldn't* get to sleep, and *if* he got an electric train it would be all right if he put in on the schoolroom floor, wouldn't it? Charlotte said she didn't think he should count on an electric train because they were terribly dear and he *must* go to sleep, and Bill said he wasn't counting on it, but it was best to have his plans made in advance in *case* he got one and not waste a lot of time next day wondering where to lay it out, and really he *couldn't* go to sleep. . . .

CHAPTER FOUR

A BLOW FOR BILL

BUT of course he did go to sleep and so, eventually, did the girls, and Christmas morning came at last, and the bells in the school chapel opposite the house were ringing, and their stockings were filled with delightful little oddments and, of course, an orange and an apple and a new half-crown in each toe.

After breakfast the whole family went into the drawing-room where Aunt Lucy had a wonderful fire blazing, to get their proper presents which were lying in large and exciting piles round the Christmas tree. Susan had kept most of her presents unopened, so she had a good big pile too. There was a cable from her mother and father from the ship, and a camera from them; there were books from Charlotte and Midge and Bill, and from Aunt Lucy and Uncle Charles—oh, wonder of wonders!—the neatest little watch. Susan was quite speechless with delight. Midge had a watch too, hers was round and Susan's was square. Charlotte had a most sumptuous new paint-box from Aunt Lucy and a writing-case from her father. Bill had opened all his other presents—and exclaimed happily over a little engine, which would drive his meccano models, from his sisters, and a very elaborate set of railway signals from Susan which she had bought the day before—and kept until the end a large and exciting-looking box which he just knew had an electric train in it—a goods one, he hoped—and rails and the transformer and . . . But when he opened it, and removed some tissue paper there were four little dolls with dangling heads and comical faces in the box.

"They're *puppets*!" cried Bill.

Aunt Lucy hung over the box, loving them. "I do hope you like them, Bill," she said. "Miss Pershore made them specially for you. We thought that you would make a good thing of them, being so good with your hands—you know, make a little stage for them, with footlights and everything."

Bill bent over the box and drew out one of the little puppets; he unwound the strings and moved the control a little—immediately the little figure —it was a clown, with a clown's sad face—danced into life, tapped his feet and waved his hands. Bill still kept his head bent down, but he couldn't help smiling at the little clown, although Susan knew that he was getting a very misty view of it, because she was too. But Bill managed to mumble, "Oh, thank you, Aunt Lucy, they're smashing. I'll go out to the garage now and see if there's any wood for my stage." And still carrying the puppet-clown, he dashed from the room.

Susan blinked hard, the girls glanced at each other and at Aunt Lucy, but apparently Aunt Lucy had realised nothing of Bill's bitter disappointment; and in a little Bill came back, everything under control, and before the family set off for church he had rigged up a temporary stage, with a bed-table and a clothes-horse, and was planning something better, and Charlotte had promised to design him a curtain, and Midge and Susan had promised to write a play for his puppets.

The Carmichaels went to the Scots Church in Pont Street, and that was a thrill for Susan too, because she had often read about it in books. They went by car, and when they came back lots of friends of Uncle Charles and Aunt Lucy came in, and their children too, who were friends of Charlotte and Midge and Bill, and the puppets were very much admired, which was encouraging for Bill, the girls felt, because he had really behaved very well over them. Susan thought that the puppets were fascinating, and longed to work them herself. Bill let her try them all in turn, and Susan began devising wild schemes of buying an electric train with her own money and swopping it with Bill for the puppets. She whispered to Midge, "How much *are* electric trains?"

"The *cheapest* is about eight pounds," Midge whispered back.

"Oh, help," said Susan. "And besides," she thought, "it's not the thing to go swopping Christmas presents. Aunt Lucy would be cut to the quick. Especially when her dearest friend has made the puppets!"

And at this moment, to everyone's relief—for they were all exceedingly hungry and Bill had reported from the kitchen that Mrs. Taylor was worrying about the bird getting overcooked, and that Chang was sitting by the oven door, howling—at this moment the dearest friend arrived.

Miss Pershore was small and very slim and elegant. Even Susan could tell that her black dress was beautifully cut and must have cost about as much as all Aunt Lucy's dresses put together, and that her pearls were real because they had a little safety-chain at the clasp. But her hair was blue.

Susan was terribly distressed for her. Surely there was *something* she could do? She whispered to Charlotte under cover of a general move to the dining-room, "Poor soul! It's terrible! Can't we tell her? She could put on a scarf, or something. We must tell her!"

"Tell who what?" said Charlotte.

"Sh, she'll hear you. Miss Pershore, of course. She has spilt something on her hair. It's *blue*."

Charlotte began to giggle. "Miss Plum won't

thank you to tell her to tie up her elegant coiffure in a hanky. It's meant to be like that."

"*Meant* to be like that?" Susan couldn't believe her ears. Really, the things that went on in London!

"Of course. That's a blue rinse," Charlotte told her, "very smart for grey hair. Although I must admit," she added, looking critically at Miss Pershore, "I must admit that it's a bit over-done this time."

Well, of course, if Charlotte said so, it must be all right for Miss Pershore to go about with blue hair, but Susan thought that it was very peculiar indeed, and often afterwards, looking back on the events of this holiday, Susan felt that the reason she never quite took to Miss Pershore was because she had blue hair.

But at the moment she hadn't much time to worry about Miss Pershore's odd taste. The dinner-table was a dream. In the centre of the table was a tiny, real Christmas tree with miniature decorations and candles and crackers and even parcels on it; trails of holly led from the tree to little golden angels (which had been painted by Charlotte and cut out by Bill on his fretsaw) holding up red candles. There were crackers piled round the foot of the tree and they were gold and green and red too. And after they had finished eating the delicious Christmas food, there was a present for everyone off the little tree

—a cigar for Uncle Charles, a china model, no more than an inch long, of a Siamese cat for Susan, a tiny compass for Bill, very pretty little hair-slides for Charlotte and Midge, and the smallest possible bottles of scent for Miss Pershore and Aunt Lucy.

In the drawing-room after dinner Miss Pershore gave Uncle Charles and Aunt Lucy their presents and gave the family a large and luscious box of French chocolates. They made appreciative exclamations and thanked her.

"Oh, this isn't your real present," said Miss Pershore. "I was going to tell you about that. You know this exhibition of toy theatres and puppets which is running in town just now? —well, there are some charming sketches, the original designs by Anna Ferdinand for the sets and characters in a toy theatre play—and she is a very well-known scene designer—and I have bought one for each of you. But of course, my pets, they're still in the exhibition! So I couldn't bring them to-day! But if you're not doing anything to-morrow morning I want you to come with me and look at them and see if you like them—or if there's another drawing you like better——"

Susan felt quite dizzy. Actually, she couldn't quite make out what the exhibition and all that was about, Midge would have to explain that to her, but the most important thing seemed to be that she, Susan, was about to own an original drawing by a famous artist!

"I think this is the most wonderful Christmas that I've ever had," said Susan, as they went to the kitchen to help Mrs. Taylor with the washing-up, "if Mummy and Daddy had been here, that is——"

"This washing-up and going out for walks while the grown-ups have forty winks rather takes the gilt off the gingerbread," murmured Midge, but nobody took any notice of her. And Chang went with them for the walk which made it more interesting, for they kept on having to rescue him from trees and dogs and other people's gardens, and consequently could go neither fast nor far. In the end even Midge admitted that the walk was a good idea for otherwise she shouldn't have been able to eat any Christmas cake when they got home. Susan said that she had been prepared to enjoy the Christmas cake anyway, but that of course it was all the better to have an appetite for it.

After tea, Miss Pershore went off to prepare for her own party. To Bill's intense satisfaction, it was to be a real evening party, going on till all hours, he told Susan. Susan couldn't get quite the same pleasure out of this information, because she trembled at the thought of the dreadful and complex pencil games that the clever Miss Pershore would have thought up for the clever Carmichaels. She went off to consult Aunt Lucy about the clothes question—did Aunt Lucy think that her blue velvet—this one that she was wearing—would be right, or should she change into her white net? Aunt Lucy thought the white net. "You'll love Miss Pershore's party," said Aunt Lucy. "She's good at parties."

Susan smiled in rather a sickly way and said politely and without much conviction that she was sure Miss Pershore was, and went off to dress.

CHAPTER FIVE

MISS PERSHORE'S PARTY

It surprised Susan very much, but Aunt Lucy was quite right—Miss Pershore *was* good at parties, although at first Susan was so frightened that she felt sick and that made her more frightened than ever, for it would be more than awkward if she were sick the minute she was inside the door. The door, incidentally, was opened by a most smart parlourmaid, and that was unnerving enough because none of Susan's mother's friends had proper maids any more, only helps or *fräuleins* or *signoritas* or *mademoiselles* or an old nanny left over or nobody at all—even Aunt Lucy had to manage that big house with Mrs. Taylor coming daily and Uncle Charles's secretary to let in the patients. And then, once they were inside, the house! It was like one of those places that you see photographed in magazines as she told Midge afterwards. You walked on priceless antique rugs and brushed past priceless antique furniture, and held your breath in case you knocked over a priceless piece of old china. Everything that could be polished was polished, every bit of silver shone. But in spite of all this magnificance, Miss Pershore was good at parties. There

were about five or six other young people there
—Daphne and John Greenwood and the Vernon
boys and a girl called Jennifer and another girl
whose name Susan didn't catch—all of whom
the Carmichaels knew, and there were one or two
grown-ups who didn't get in the way. They
began by guessing advertisements pinned round
the drawing-room and Susan won that; she
always won that advertisement game because she
liked reading advertisements, and always believed
them too. So that very much restored her self-
confidence. Then they played beetle and then
they had supper—with wonderful food—and
after that they played really good games like
sardines, and murder and hide-and-seek in the
dark. Susan always loved hide-and-seek in the
dark, although she trembled for Miss Pershore's
priceless ornaments. She needn't have worried
because Miss Pershore had carefully put away her
real treasures before the party began, but as
Susan didn't know this she admired Miss Pershore's apparent casualness.

"Go where you like," said Miss Pershore,
"under the beds if you like—only not on the top
floor if you don't mind because you might
wander into my workroom by mistake and get
paint or something on those heavenly dresses——"

She switched off the lights and the company
crept off. Susan was "he," much to her trepida-
tion. She in any case always managed to work

herself into a frenzy at hide-and-seek in the dark, creeping about in a state of delicious terror; to be "he" increased her terror. However, she successfully sought out the others, except the girl whose name she didn't know. Midge was "he" next time and Susan went off to hide in peace. She giggled a little with Bill, knocked into, she thought, Charlotte and went upstairs. However, the excitement or something must have gone to her head because without thinking, indeed without realising, she crept up the second flight of stairs, and hid behind the first open door she found. There was absolute stillness round her —at first; then she began to hear little rustlings, creaks and murmurings; her heart began again to go thump, thump. Far away downstairs she could hear the comfortable sound of the telephone ringing; she heard a muffled shriek and a rather hysterical giggle, quickly stilled, and again there was silence. Then she heard the sound she was dreading—soft footsteps coming upstairs. She flattened herself against the wall, trembling. The footsteps came nearer—the door was suddenly pushed against her, she choked back a yell—and to her astonishment, the light snapped on. From behind the door she saw Miss Pershore walk across the room. Susan was opening her mouth to speak to her when Miss Pershore opened the door of a big cupboard and stepped inside.

Susan grinned to herself. "Very sporting of

Miss Plum to join the game," she thought, "but for goodness' sake, why did she put the light on?" She was just going to nip out from behind her door to put it out, when a call came from below, "Come out, come out, wherever you be——"

"Oh, good," thought Susan, "I wasn't found ... Miss Pershore!" she called. "You can come out, Midge hasn't found us." There was no reply. Rather puzzled, she walked over to the cupboard. Without it making any impression on her, she half-noticed that she was in a sort of workroom fitted up with a carpenter's bench and with puppets in various stages of completion hanging here and there. She opened the cupboard door. "Miss Pershore——" she began, and stopped, amazed. The cupboard was empty. "Oh, help," thought Susan, "I'm going dotty," and she quickly shut the cupboard door and ran downstairs.

The party was gathered in the dining-room having ices and jellies and trifles and lemonade. "Come on, Susie," said Midge, as Susan came in, "not like you to be late for food. Where were you hiding? You were the only one I didn't find. Don't be too long; Miss Pershore's going to give us a puppet-show—she's getting the puppets ready now. What d'you want—an ice?"

Susan took the ice from Midge, who was too busy helping to hand round the food to notice Susan's unusual silence. Susan wondered a little if she would manage to eat an ice, because she was feeling extremely queer. Was she seeing things? How did Miss Plum manage to disappear like that? However, as the ice rapidly disappeared too Susan felt that there couldn't be *much* the matter with her. And after she had watched Miss Plum's marvellous skill in manipulating the puppets in a little play of *Hansel and Gretel*, she felt that nothing was beyond Miss Plum's powers. Disappearing in a cupboard would be child's play for her, Susan thought, and wouldn't have been surprised if she had disappeared in a cloud of smoke before the very eyes of the assembled company.

"Besides," she said to herself, coming back to earth slightly, "she probably slipped out again when I wasn't looking."

All the same, when the good-byes were being said and everyone was exclaiming what a marvellous party it had been, some niggle of curiosity made Susan say, "Thank you very much for having me, Miss Pershore, it was the best party I've ever been at, and Midge didn't find *you* at hide-and-seek."

Miss Pershore said in her charming way, "Was Midge looking for me in the dark?" I wasn't playing."

"Oh, weren't you? I thought I saw you going into a press to hide," said Susan.

"Into a *press*?" said Miss Pershore, bewildered.

"She means a cupboard, Miss Pershore," translated Midge. "Scots people call a cupboard a press, you know."

Susan was wishing ardently that there was a convenient press into which *she* could disappear. Miss Pershore gave her a look which sent shivers up and down her back. Then Miss Pershore smiled and said lightly, "All those games must have inflamed your imagination, Susan," and she turned away and was busy shaking hands with her other departing guests.

"*What* inflamed your imagination, Susan?" said Bill, who didn't miss much, as they ran home to their own house.

"Ugh, nothing," said Susan, who was feeling a little uncomfortable. "Sometimes I think I'm slightly potty."

"I'd be the last to deny that," said Midge. "And you do rather suffer from an inflamed imagination."

"'Inflamed imagination!'" thought Susan. "She *did* go into that press—cupboard." But as Susan had by this time realised that she herself had been out-of-bounds, she felt the less said about cupboards and workrooms and hide-and-seek in the dark the better. So she didn't mention it to the rest of the family as they climbed upstairs to bed, yawning.

"I do think it's sad when Christmas Day is over," said Midge, "and Boxing Day is always such an anti-climax."

CHAPTER SIX

TWOPENCE COLOURED

APART altogether from the ballet, Boxing Day was to prove anything but an anti-climax.

To begin with, Miss Pershore took them into town in her car, and as it was the first time that Susan had ever ridden in a Rolls Royce, she sat back and enjoyed the unaccustomed luxury to the full.

The exhibition was in Albemarle Street, and had practically no visitors but themselves that quiet Boxing Day morning.

On the ground floor were the exhibits concerning the theatre proper—valuable first editions of plays, prompt copies used by famous actors of the past, old playbills, old prints. Some of them had been lent by the governors of Wichwood College, which had been founded by an actor, which was particularly interesting for Susan and the Carmichaels.

In a room upstairs there were the toy theatres and the puppets. Of course they all went straight to the sketches for the toy theatre play. The one which Miss Pershore had chosen for Susan was the sketch of a serving-maid with a gay, impudent face; Bill's was a highwayman in a scarlet cloak; Midge's a dainty little waiting-woman and Charlotte's was the beautiful heroine. They all had a little red disc in the corner which meant SOLD. The Carmichaels and Susan were charmed with them.

They scarcely had words to thank Miss Pershore and felt extremely important to be the owners of drawings which were actually in a real exhibition; and that naturally made up for having to wait until the exhibition was over before getting them into their possession.

Miss Pershore told them some interesting things about puppets and toy theatres—that though toy theatres had fallen into a decline until recently, over a hundred years ago nearly all the successful plays of the proper London stage were issued in special sheets of scenery and characters for performance in the toy theatre—"a penny plain and twopence coloured." Susan said that she never knew before where that phrase, "a penny plain and twopence coloured" came from though she had heard it often. Miss Pershore also told them that puppets were very, very old in origin and known all over the world, and that one, Captain Pod, in 1599, was the first puppet-showman known by name in England. "Fancy, 1599!" they said, and went to admire the puppets.

Susan was spellbound by the little figures

arranged in miniature stage sets round the room —the Mad Hatter's Tea-party, and the Owl and the Pussy-cat and Pinocchio with Gepetto; there were plenty of funny puppets and ugly puppets, there were beautiful puppets, like the Sleeping Beauty and the Lady Greensleeves and little ballet dancers.

They were particularly intrigued by the stand where there was a demonstration of how to make a puppet. Susan sighed, and longed to have a try at making one, only, she said, she knew too well what the result would be like because she never could do anything with her hands, and Bill promised that when he had more time he would try to make one for her, only it would have to be a glove puppet because he didn't think he could manage the strings.

"And now," said Miss Pershore, "if you can tear yourselves away from these puppets, we'll go downstairs and have some coffee or lemonade or something."

They went down the handsome staircase, and the girl in charge of the exhibition on the ground floor came out to have a word with Miss Pershore. Susan wandered back into the exhibition to look again at an old playbill that had interested her:

THEATRE ROYAL, HAYMARKET

Mr. CHARLES KEAN

Will appear TO-NIGHT (for the first and
only time) as

SIR EDWARD MORTIMER

in

THE IRON CHEST

And on Friday

in

MACBETH

Positively his last appearance in London this
Season

As she slipped into the room, a man who was
standing by one of the cases at the far end of the
room, dropped the lid of the case with a slight
crash.

He glanced across at Susan with a rueful expression. He was a youngish man, plump and
good-looking in a seedy sort of way, with wavy
hair worn too long. Susan thought, from her
vast experience, that he looked like an actor.

"Oh, dear," he said with a charming smile,
"how very clumsy of me!"

Susan walked over towards him. "Can I help
you?" she said.

The man looked a little startled. Then he smiled again.

"Well, if you would be so very kind," he said. "It is so difficult to hold the lid of the case up and move the books at the same time——"

"I'll hold the lid," said Susan.

"Thank you, my dear," said the man, and while Susan held the glass lid, he slipped out two little old books from the strings that held them open.

"I suppose you're moving them to another case," said Susan.

"Why, yes, my dear!" he said. "I'm moving them. They don't look much, do they?" he said. "But they are very valuable, very valuable indeed. It's a first edition of *The Tragedy of the Duchess of Malfi*, you know. We must take the greatest care of them." He put them tenderly into his pocket and gave Susan a courtly bow. "A thousand thanks, dear child," he said.

Susan felt that she should at least have curtseyed in return, but contented herself with smiling and giving him an awkward little duck of her head. She turned to her playbill, and the man moved to the door. He stood aside to let the girl in charge come in, and with another bow to Susan, he went out.

Midge put her head round the door, looking for Susan.

"Oh, there you are," she said. "Come on,

we're going down to the restaurant for elevenses."
They joined the others in the hall, and they were
all moving off to the staircase which led to the
restaurant below when there came a terrible
shriek from the exhibition room. The whole
party rushed back into the room.

The girl in charge was standing at the far end,
staring at one of the cases in horror, and shrieking,
"Help! Help! Thieves! *Ralph Roister Doister's*
gone! The only known copy——! *The Duchess
of Malfi's* gone! They were here a moment ago
and they've been stolen! Help! Help! They're
gone!" She turned to Miss Pershore and her
party who were making anxious, twittering,
enquiring noises, all except Susan, who was
staring at the girl wild-eyed, and feeling terribly
sick.

"We must telephone the police," said Miss
Pershore, and she ran towards the reception
desk in the middle of the room where there was
a telephone.

"Yes, yes!" cried the girl, "phone the police!
It was that man! I passed him as I came in! He
must have taken them!"

Bill said, "He's just gone out! I saw him take
his coat and hat off the stand."

"Come on!" cried Susan. "Bill, Midge, Charlotte, come *on*—he can't have gone far." She
ran out of the house and down the stairs with
the Carmichaels at her heels. She looked up and

down the street. It was almost deserted, that morning.

"There he is!" cried Bill. "Just turning into Piccadilly——"

The four of them ran down Albemarle Street and into Piccadilly. They saw the man walking in the direction of Piccadilly Circus, and then he disappeared.

"He's gone up Bond Street!" said Charlotte.

"I hope nobody sees us," panted Susan as they ran. "We must look daft."

"It doesn't much matter *how* daft you look in London," Bill panted back, "there's always someone who looks dafter."

"Well, but four of us," said Susan, "tearing along like maniacs." But she ran on, all the same.

At the corner of Bond Street she stopped and wailed, "Oh, we've lost him! He got on to that bus!"

"It's stopping for the lights!" cried Bill. "Come *on*, we can just catch it!"

They ran across Bond Street and bundled on to the bus which was just moving off. The conductor grumbled at them amiably, and they beamed at him, and fell into seats, panting.

"Where is he?" whispered Midge. "I can't see him."

"He must have gone upstairs," said Susan.

"And now what do we do?" said Charlotte.

"I must say, I think we've acted very rashly chasing after him like this. We should have waited for the police."

"I didn't *dare* wait for the police," said Susan. "We've *got* to get those books back. At least I have. I can't face the police!"

"What *are* you talking about, Susie?" said Charlotte. "Why so coy about the police? You'd think you were an old lag."

Susan began to blush. "I'm not an old lag but I'm a new one," she said miserably. "I—I *helped* him."

"You *helped* him?" repeated Charlotte. Midge and Bill gaped.

Susan nodded. "I thought he was an attendant," she said in a small voice. "I held the case open for him while he took out the books."

"But how on earth could you think he was an attendant?" said Midge, beginning to giggle.

"Ugh, I don't know. He just looked so much at home I never imagined for a moment he was *stealing* the books. He must have had a skeleton key or something and unlocked the case before I appeared. And he was perfectly at ease and talked about one of the books. . . . So you see, I really don't want to face the police with that story. I want to get the books back."

The conductor came hovering up for the fares. The Carmichaels and Susan went into a huddle; the conductor got bored and went upstairs.

"Oh, goodness," whispered Charlotte, "what do we ask for?"

"Better ask for sixpenny ones," whispered Bill, "to be on the safe side."

"But if the man gets off soon that's a lot of money wasted," whispered Susan.

"Well, but if he doesn't get off, we can't keep *on* asking for threeha'penny ones," whispered Midge, "the conductor will think we're potty."

"It's really much easier in books where you just leap into a taxi and say, ' Follow that bus!'" said Susan.

"We'd better get sixpenny ones, I suppose," said Charlotte, "but I'll expect to have this money refunded. Two shillings indeed!"

"Not two shillings surely," said Bill. "I go for half."

So when the conductor came back, Charlotte said, "Three sixpenny ones and a half, please."

The conductor grinned at them. "We only go as far as Victoria," he said. "Where d'*you* want to go?"

"Oh, Victoria will do quite nicely," said Charlotte, feeling silly.

The conductor gave her the three threeha'penny tickets and one penny one and went off up the bus, still grinning.

"Well, he's got to get off at Victoria, seeing the bus stops there," said Midge. "I hope we don't lose him in the crowd round the station."

"You're sure he hasn't got off already?" said Charlotte.

"He hasn't. I've been watching," said Bill calmly. "I don't expect he has any idea that we're after him, and you're the only one he knows, Susie. You keep your face turned away."

"How can I watch out for him with my face turned away?" said Susan.

"Oh, pretend to be blowing your nose or something—hide your face with your handkerchief," said Bill, who was enjoying himself.

"What do we do when he does get off?" said Charlotte.

"We get off too?" suggested Susan.

"Yes, but after that, you dope," said Charlotte. "Honestly, I think this was a most ill-advised expedition."

By this time the bus was swinging round from Piccadilly into Grosvenor Gardens. "Oh, dear," said Charlotte, "we'll soon be at Victoria. What are we to do?"

"We'll see when the time comes," said Midge soothingly.

When the time came, the man gave them very little choice. Whether he had tumbled to the fact that he was being followed—which wouldn't, as a matter of fact, have taken much brain, for his pursuers were as obvious as a pack of hounds in an open field—or not, he acted very speedily, darted across the road, dodging taxis, and disappeared. "Oh, bother," exclaimed Bill, "he's gone into the Underground! If he once gets into a tube, we've lost him. Come *on*!"

All four swarmed across the road, dodging taxis in their turn. Susan lost her nerve at one point and dithered backwards and forwards and was shouted at by a taxi-driver, but eventually made up on her more traffic-conscious cousins, who were by this time running down the stairs to the Underground and along a subway into a confusing jumble of barriers, ticket-machines and crowds of people who all seemed to be going in the opposite direction from them.

"Quick!" said Bill, "I can still see him—this way—to ' Eastbound Trains.'"

"What about tickets?" panted Charlotte.

"*Don't* stop for tickets," said Bill. "We might lose him."

"What about the ticket-collector at the barrier?" said Susan anxiously, but no one answered and she was obliged to hurry after the others past the ticket man as if she were in the habit of pushing through barriers without a ticket every day of her life. Then they clattered down the stairs and were in time to see their quarry boarding a train. They bundled in after him.

"Don't let him see you, Susan," begged Bill. "Keep your head down and do cover your face with your handkerchief. He doesn't know us—we'll keep an eye on him."

"He must have seen us by now, I should think," murmured Midge. "We're a not inconspicuous party."

The man got off at Charing Cross and the chase started again. Up stairs, down escalators, round corners—to the Bakerloo line. Susan was in a perfect daze, thinking sadly that under happier circumstances she would have loved all those tubes and escalators.

"Steady *on*," said Midge, "if we're not careful we'll over-run him and get there before he does."

"Get *where*?" murmured Charlotte hopelessly.

"But if we lose him in the Underground we've lost him for ever," said Bill anxiously.

The man boarded a Northbound train, and so did his pursuers. "Mind the doo-oo-ers!" called the guard.

The car fortunately was busy. The Carmichaels and Susan stood in a bunch at one end, furtively watching their man, who was strap-hanging farther along.

"I think he has spotted us," said Bill, annoyed. "I've caught his eye twice. I bet he gets off at Piccadilly Circus and tries to lose us. Be ready!"

They were ready. The man *did* get off at Piccadilly Circus, and they were after him. Up stairs, along more passages and then to the escalators.

"Oo-oo-ooh!" said Susan when she saw the height of the escalators.

"Come on!" said Midge. "You can't stand there enjoying yourself. You've got to walk up or he'll get miles ahead."

At the top, they had him well in sight. "Time we closed in on him," said Bill. With their eyes on their quarry they forged on.

"Hey!" came an angry shout. "What about your tickets?" Guiltily, they stopped half-way through the barrier. They had completely forgotten about tickets. The ticket collector eyed them. "Think London Transport was going to give you a free ride for Boxing Day?" he asked. The gathering crowd greeted this sally with titters. Susan began to blush.

"Of course not," said Charlotte with dignity, "we were in a hurry at the other end."

"Seemed to be in a bit of a hurry at this end too," said the ticket collector. "Where did you come from?"

"Victoria," said Charlotte. "Three and a half from Victoria please."

"Tenpence-ha'penny," said the ticket collector.

Charlotte began hunting in her purse. "Midge," she muttered, "have you any money?" They both began burrowing in their purses. The ticket collector leant back in his seat with an exaggerated air of patience.

"Can you see him?" whispered Bill to Susan in an agony, "I think I've lost him."

"Yes, I can see him," said Susan, standing on

tiptoe and craning her neck. "Oh, help, he's gone!"

But they were through at last. "This way!" said Susan and darted to the right. "He went out this exit—I think——"

They stood disconsolate at the exit marked "Haymarket." Their man was nowhere to be seen. "Are you sure it was this one, Susan?" said Midge.

Susan ran on a few steps and looked irresolutely at the next exit—"Piccadilly South Side." The tube station was a hopeless confusion to Susan. Streams of people were coming and going; streams of people were moving round the vast circle; there were shop-windows and lights and the clanking noise of the escalators, telephone kiosks and heat; there were countless exits— "Shaftesbury Avenue," "Regent Street North Side." A rabbit warren in a nightmare must look like this, she thought. "I *thought* it was that one," she said, "but they all look the same. Oh, help!"

At that moment, amazingly, their quarry reappeared at the exit marked "Haymarket."

"There he *is*!" shouted Susan, and she ran up to him. The Carmichaels closed in on him.

The man stopped, took off his soft black hat and gave Susan another courtly bow. "Can I do something for you?" he enquired with his charming smile.

"Yes," said Susan fiercely, "you can give me back those books I stupidly helped you to steal!"

"And you needn't think you can get away," said Bill, "because we're four to one."

"And if you don't hand them over," said Charlotte, "we'll call a policeman."

"And when the policeman finds the books on you," said Midge, "you'll go to prison."

The man raised a quizzical eyebrow.

"My dear child," he said, "not even a policeman could find any books on me. Because I have no books."

"Of course you have," said Susan, "I saw you put them in your pocket."

"Well, if it will stop this rather unpleasant scene, and this rather unpleasant talk of policemen," said the man, "you're welcome to look in my pockets."

Susan stared at him, doubtfully.

"Go on, look!" said the man, smiling at her.

"Bill, feel his pockets," said Charlotte.

Bill slapped the pockets of the man's overcoat "Nothing there," he muttered.

"Go on, do the job properly, look in my jacket pockets," said the man, obligingly, and began turning out his pockets. "Look, keys, wallet, handkerchief," he said, "but no books I assure you."

Bill began to shuffle his feet in an embarrassed way. Midge put her foot unobtrusively on a slip of paper which had fluttered unnoticed to the ground.

"I'm very sorry," Bill mumbled.

"Don't mention it," said the man. "Now may I go? Without a stain on my character?" Once more he raised his hat, and turned away towards the trains.

Susan and the Carmichaels watched him go. Midge stooped down and picked up the piece of paper.

"I could *howl*," said Susan.

"I suppose we'd better phone Miss Plum and tell her it's no good," said Charlotte.

"Was it the wrong man?" said Bill. "Where are the books? He was so jaunty about it. Do we still follow him?"

"Oh, I don't think we need," said Midge airily. "Follow me, instead." She marched off to the Haymarket exit, and the others followed, twittering.

"Where are you going, Midge?"

"What's the idea?"

"Midge, *where* are you going?"

"I'm going to the left-luggage office," said Midge, "it's just up here."

"I suppose we've all gone daft," said Susan hopelessly.

Midge didn't answer, but walked resolutely down a short flight of steps to the left-luggage office. She handed the slip of paper to the man in charge. The man disappeared among the shelves for an instant then came back with something which he handed to Midge. It was two little old books tied together with a piece of string.

They were the heroes of the day when they got back to Albemarle Street and the theatre exhibition. The girl in charge was almost hysterical with relief and gratitude. Miss Pershore was most impressed, took them down to the restaurant and plied them with questions and lemonade.

"The bit *I* can't make out," said Susan, "was how Midge knew the books were in the left-luggage office."

"I just used my brains," said Midge. "I remembered that there was a left-luggage office in the Haymarket exit, and it was quite obvious that he had got rid of the books when he was so cock-sure about letting us search him. So when I saw the ticket fall I wondered if that was how he'd got rid of them. And it was."

"It was the most exciting morning I've ever had in my life," said Charlotte. "Not enjoyable, but exciting. And you all owe me fourpence-ha'penny, except Bill, who owes me tuppence-ha'penny."

"*My* only regret," said Bill, "was that none of it happened in Joe's area. It's the first time we've ever been mixed up in anything like this, and it has to happen out of Joe's area."

"I suppose it *was* quite exciting," said Susan, "now that it's all over and there's no harm done. But it has taken a lot out of me. I don't think I'll ever be the same again. And I will never, as long as I live, try to help anyone again!"

"Oh, Susan," said Miss Pershore, laughing, "don't say that! Your helping hand won't always be put to such base uses, I hope. You won't always be having such a twopence-coloured kind of morning as this one."

It was a twopence-coloured kind of evening too. None of her cousins had prepared Susan for Covent Garden Opera House—for the simple reason that none of them had ever been there. Uncle Charles parked the car, and they walked the short distance to the theatre. Susan, while always ready for the unexpected in London, couldn't help saying to Midge, in a low voice, lest Uncle Charles's feelings should be hurt, "Midge, are we going the right way? I keep tripping over orange boxes and bits of cabbage."

"Well, of course," said Midge, "this is Covent Garden Market, you know, where the fruit and flowers and vegetables are sold. Charlotte and I got up at five one day last summer and came up to see the market. I didn't recover for weeks and it certainly wasn't worth the effort because all the flowers were in boxes and it wasn't a bit like what I'd expected."

"Funny place to have an opera house," said Susan, rather expecting that the cabbage stalks and fruit baskets would stray into the theatre, so that when she stepped inside, the contrast between the rather squalid scenes without, and the glories within took her breath away, and she never really got it back the whole evening. The red carpets, the gold, the glittering chandeliers as they went upstairs, and then the great theatre itself delighted her. Thanks to Miss Pershore, they had wonderful seats in the front row of the Grand Tier; they could see up and down and round about, apart altogether from having a perfectly splendid view of the stage itself. This, thought Susan with satisfaction, is something like a theatre, for so many things that you had read about and *read* about were apt not to be so wonderful as you had imagined. She hadn't really imagined anything about the ballet itself for she had very little, if any, idea what to expect. Certainly she hadn't expected to love every moment of it, to feel practically like crying—only naturally you couldn't when you were fourteen— when Cinderella danced alone with her broom, or to feel like standing up and cheering when she swept off in triumph to the ball in her exquisite coach.

"Much better than a pantomime," she whispered to Bill as the grown-ups led them down a flight of steps to another splendid part of the theatre, which was called the crush bar, for iced lemonade and cakes after Act 1; and as Bill had nearly fallen off his seat laughing at the Ugly Sisters, he was inclined to agree with her.

And after it was over and they came out into the frosty night, still bewitched by the dancing and the colour and the music, Uncle Charles obligingly motored them round and round Piccadilly Circus to show Susan the lights—and Bill too, incidentally, for, as he said with glee, it wasn't often that *he* was gallivanting about the West End at ten o'clock at night. Then they went round Trafalgar Square and saw the floodlit fountains and the fairy lights twinkling in the giant Christmas tree sent by the people of Norway; and so home down Whitehall and over Westminster Bridge.

"I've never, *never* had such a wonderful evening," Susan told Aunt Lucy and Uncle Charles earnestly when they were again at home, enjoying another of those delicious suppers round the fire that Aunt Lucy seemed to have a genius for producing.

Midge yawned. "Penny plain to-morrow, I'm afraid," she said.

CHAPTER SEVEN

CHANG BREAKS THE ICE

NEXT morning, which was Sunday, the girls were awakened by rapturous shouts from Bill. "Snow! Snow! There's snow on the ground!"

Susan opened her eyes and indeed that curious, mysterious, exciting white light which meant snow, filled the room. Charlotte came in declaiming:

" *When men were all asleep the snow came flying
In large white flakes falling on the city brown.*"

Even Midge got out of bed and went to the window.

"Huh!" she said in disgust, "half an inch, I should say—if that," and went back to bed again.

"But it's lying!" said Bill. "It was freezing yesterday, you know—there was ice on the pond in the park and on our own little pond in the orchard. I thought we'd get some skating, but it'll be much more fun if we have snow. We'll take the toboggan up to the golf-course hill— *what* a good thing I mended it!"

"Darling Bill," Midge grumbled from under the blankets, "we can't toboggan down the golf-course hill on half an inch of snow."

"But there's more coming," said Bill impatiently, dancing up and down at the window. "*Look* at the sky!"

"Later, later," murmured Midge.

"Ugh, I *hope* there's more snow," said Susan. "Do you know, Bill, I haven't gone sledging for two years!"

"Sledging?" said Bill. "Neither have I. What is sledging?"

"And you call yourself a Scot," said Charlotte. "A sledge is a toboggan. And go and get your dressing-gown on for goodness' sake—you'll get your death of cold!"

"I'm going to get dressed," said Bill, "and go out. You don't think I'm going to frowst indoors when there's snow?"

After breakfast, before it was time to get ready for church, Midge and Susan put on Wellington boots and went out too, mainly for the pleasure of seeing their footprints in the untrodden snow on the lawn. Bill was in the garage, making sure that the toboggan was in first-class condition. Charlotte was helping Aunt Lucy indoors.

"Look at Chang," said Susan fondly, "behaving like a lunatic!" Chang was prancing about, darting here and there, chasing his tail and altogether behaving in a very skittish fashion. "He loves snow. Don't you think it's odd that a cat should like snow?"

"I think it's odd that a *Siamese* should like

snow," Midge said, "but we had an ordinary cat once who loved snow."

With Chang cavorting round them they walked across the garden. It was a very pretty garden, framed by the big trees of the park. A little path led across the lane to the vegetable garden and the little orchard with the pond in one corner. It looked much less savage territory than it had seemed on Christmas Eve when Susan and Bill had stumbled across it.

"It's just like a Christmas card to-day," said Midge happily as they went into the orchard.

"By the way," said Susan, "talking of Christmas cards, here's the snow."

Midge thought this over for a second, but finally admitted defeat. "I haven't the faintest idea what you're talking about," she said.

"Goodness," said Susan, "the snow we were going to push Aunt Lucy into, of course, so that she would get dangerously ill."

"Oh," said Midge, not very enthusiastically, "were we?"

"Only," said Susan, looking round, "I don't think there's quite enough."

"How right you are," said Midge thankfully. "There isn't enough to push Chang into!"

Even as the words left her lips, Chang came bounding happily over the short grass under the trees and bounded equally happily on to the pond, which, indeed, under its layer of snow looked no different from the grass. There was a crackling of thin ice, and Chang disappeared.

Susan ran to the edge of the pond in terror. "Chang! *Chang!*" she shouted. Then she turned to Midge. "Go and get a ladder and a rope! And get Aunt Lucy!" And then she plunged into the pond.

Midge sped off to the house. She couldn't imagine what old Susie thought she was going to do with a ladder and a rope, but she had no doubt that Aunt Lucy would be useful.

Aunt Lucy was telephoning to say good-bye to Miss Pershore who was going to Paris for a couple of days and to thank her for a nice party. When Midge came charging in—bringing rather a lot of snow on her boots, incidentally, although that was nothing to what was brought in later —shouting, "Aunt Lucy! Help! Quick! Susie's in the pond! And Chang's in the pond!" Aunt Lucy flung down the receiver and ran out, just as she was, coatless and wearing thin slippers. When she reached the pond, Susan was kneeling down in it, thrashing about her with her hands.

"Susan!" cried Aunt Lucy, "Come out at once. You'll get your death of cold!"

Susan's teeth were chattering so violently that she could scarcely speak, but she managed to mumble out, "I c-c-can't . . . c-c-ome . . . out. Chang's . . . d-d-dead . . . and d-d-drowned . . . I . . . m-m-must find . . . him."

"My darling child," said Aunt Lucy, "Chang passed me as I came up the garden. He was streaking for home and dripping wet and he looked like a particularly revolting rat. So you can come out."

"Oh, Aunt L-L-Lucy how wonderful!" chattered Susan, and she stumbled to her feet. Then a bright idea darted into her head. She sank to her knees again. "B-b-but I c-c-can't c-c-come out," she said. "I'm s-sort of s-stuck."

"Well," said Aunt Lucy, "I'm certainly not coming in, so you had better get unstuck."

Susan struggled to her feet once more, and after falling once or twice, for her feet were indeed embedded in deep mud, she did manage to come nearer the edge. She held out a hand.

"C-c-could you g-g-give m-m-me a h-h-hand?" she said.

Aunt Lucy glanced down at her by now sodden slippers and shrugged. "Oh, well," she said, and came a little nearer and firmly grasped Susan's icy hand. She pulled. Susan pulled. "Susan!" shrieked Aunt Lucy. She slipped on the frozen snow and plunged headlong into the pond.

Susan was aghast when she saw what she had done, and she was too stiff and numb with cold herself to be much help. Aunt Lucy, gasping, drenched and shivering, struggled to her feet, and like a couple of rather seedy old sea-lions the two clambered out.

"R-r-run, Susan, r-run to the house," said Aunt Lucy.

"I c-c-can't," said Susan, "I c-c-can't move my f-f-feet——"

"If you emptied the w-w-water out of your b-b-boots," Aunt Lucy began. She helped Susan to pull off her boots and Susan poured out a stream of muddy, dirty, icy water. Then she put her boots on again and began to lumber back to the house. She had never felt so cold in her life. She began to remember horrible stories of frostbite and wondered how soon she could expect her nose and fingers and toes to drop off. She had no feeling at all in any of them—for all she knew her toes might be off already. She was just going to ask Aunt Lucy what she thought about this, when Aunt Lucy took her by the wrist and began to run with her towards the house, and Susan had to use all her concentration for keeping upright. When they reached the house, Aunt Lucy pushed her into the kitchen and told her to get her clothes off and started giving orders for hot baths and hot-water bottles. Midge was kneeling on the floor near the fire, rubbing Chang with a big warm towel while Chang howled piteously whenever his head appeared out of the folds.

"Oh, gracious!" Midge said when Susan stumbled in. "Another one!" Chang took advantage of the diversion created by his mistress's arrival to leap out of Midge's arms with a final protesting growl. He sat down by the boiler, angrily licking himself.

Susan stood helplessly dripping in the middle of the floor.

"Am I supposed to rub you down too?" said Midge. "If I am, you had better take your clothes off."

"I c-c-can't," said Susan. "My f-f-fingers are n-n-numb."

Midge began to undress her, and gradually the feeling began to steal back into Susan's limbs in a very painful way. She took off her stockings with some anxiety, rather expecting to shake a few toes out of them; they were, however, all intact, which was a considerable relief. Aunt Lucy meantime had a hot bath ready for her, and Mrs. Taylor was filling two hot-water bottles.

"Surely I don't have to go to *bed*?" objected Susan. "And what about you, Aunt Lucy? You'll be getting pneumonia!" Her conscience pricked her a little as she thought of it. "You have the bath," she said magnanimously.

"I'm certainly going to have a bath, my pet," said Aunt Lucy, "for we smell disgustingly. Really, that pond *can't* be clean in spite of what Uncle Charles says. But the top-floor bath is ready for you, and then into bed with you. You can get up for tea."

By tea-time it wasn't Susan that was up, but

her temperature. Throughout the afternoon the family had dropped into her room at intervals to commiserate with her, and the cause of all the trouble came and settled down with her under the eiderdown when Aunt Lucy wasn't looking. Susan was very glad to see them all, but she couldn't help wishing that she was in better trim, as she put it, for visitors. Really, she felt very peculiar indeed, and in spite of two hot-water bottles, four blankets, an eiderdown and Chang, she just couldn't get warm. Aunt Lucy came in and out, looking extremely healthy, which was very grudging, Susan felt, after all the trouble she had taken; and not long before tea Aunt Lucy glanced at Susan's flushed face and went and fetched a thermometer.

"Ugh, I shouldn't pay any attention to a *thermometer*," said Susan desperately when she saw it. "I always get the most terrific temperatures for absolutely nothing at all. They don't mean anything and go down just as quickly I——"

Aunt Lucy pushed the thermometer in as Susan was taking breath for some more arguments. "Keep your mouth closed, darling," she said, "if you have no temperature then of course you can get up."

Susan, corked up with the thermometer, glanced up at Aunt Lucy. Was Aunt Lucy being perhaps a wee bit malicious, Susan couldn't help wondering? After all, she was sort of smiling, and there was really nothing to smile about. . . . But on the other hand, surely Aunt Lucy couldn't have guessed that Susan had pulled her into the pond deliberately? And a lot of good it had been, she thought, with Aunt Lucy standing there, bursting with rude health and herself lying burning and shivering and her feet as cold as ice.

Aunt Lucy took out the thermometer and read it and tut-tutted at Susan. And there was evidently no question of Susan's getting up; in fact, she spent the evening feeling more and more ill, and at night Aunt Lucy changed beds with Midge so that she could keep an eye on her and supply her with the various potions provided by Uncle Charles; and the night passed for Susan very miserably and slowly, and in the morning there was still absolutely no question of her getting up, and that was particularly galling because there was the most beautiful thick white blanket of snow covering everything.

Midge and Bill bewailed the harshness of fate with her.

"It's sickening, maddening, disgusting," Midge said. "We haven't had a decent fall of snow like this for years. And it's freezing again now, too —perfect for tobogganing."

"I've oiled the toboggan and polished it and everything," sighed Bill. "It's rotten you can't come, Susan."

Aunt Lucy came in with some orange juice for the invalid. "Uncle Charles thinks you'll soon be better," she said comfortingly, "and perhaps the snow won't be gone. The last time we had real snow it lasted for six weeks. I *dread* the thought of it."

This was a quite incomprehensible attitude to Susan and Midge and Bill, for they could think of nothing more wonderful than six weeks of snow and ice. But grown-ups, they knew, had queer ways of looking at things.

Charlotte opened the bedroom door a cautious two inches, and with her hand over her mouth mumbled, "Poor old Susan! Rotten for you! Have you plenty to read? Oh, good! I've brought you a book about puppets that Miss Pershore lent me which you might like." She threw the book on the bed. "Well, come on, then, Midge and Bill—the Greenwoods went past ages ago with their toboggan."

"What's the matter with Charlotte?" Susan murmured to Midge.

Midge grinned. "Terrified she gets a germ," she whispered.

"From me?" said Susan, amazed. "But I haven't got germs, I've only got a chill."

Midge was still grinning. "Charlotte's always like this when any of us are ill," she said. "Even if it's only chilblains. She'll make a wonderful nurse, won't she?" and she got up from Susan's bed and prepared leisurely to depart.

"*Do* hurry," called Charlotte from outside the door. "'Bye, Susie!"

"Oh, Charlotte," called Aunt Lucy.

Charlotte reluctantly put the top of her golden head and half an eye round the door.

"Oh, Charlotte," said Aunt Lucy, "don't you think that this would be an awfully good chance for you to get some nursing practice? I have rather a lot to do to-day, and Susan isn't infectious, but she does need a bit of looking after."

Susan opened her mouth to protest, then shut it again. It wasn't exactly what she had planned but, after all, one patient was as good as another to show Aunt Lucy what a wonderful nurse Charlotte was.

The nurse was showing considerable reluctance to get started. "But, Aunt Lucy, we were going up to the golf-course to toboggan!" she wailed.

"Yes, I know, darling," said Aunt Lucy sweetly, "I know you'll miss the fun, but it's not much fun for poor Susan either, is it? And it does seem rather a good opportunity for you——"

"But I might catch something," said Charlotte sulkily.

"Well, darling," said Aunt Lucy, "nurses have got to chance that, haven't they? Come along and I'll give you a white overall and tell you what you must do."

Aunt Lucy bustled off the still protesting Charlotte.

Midge and Bill grinned at each other. "The only one *I'm* sorry for," said Midge, "is poor old Susie."

"Why poor old Susie?" said Susan in alarm. But Midge and Bill bade her good-bye without explaining and went off on their tobogganing expedition, still grinning.

Susan was right about one thing. Charlotte looked ravishingly pretty in the white coat, although as a matter of fact you couldn't see half of her face because she had tied a handkerchief three-cornerways across her mouth.

"What on earth's that for?" said Susan.

Charlotte glanced at her rather malevolently. "Nurses wear masks, don't they?" she said.

"Well, yes," said Susan, "when they're helping at an operation. Or when they're feeding a baby. But that's to protect the baby."

"This is to protect me," said Charlotte. "I don't want any of your horrible germs!" She came round to the bedside table to put a jug on it, accidentally kicking the bed as she came. It jarred right through poor Susan's aching head. Charlotte went on, "Aunt Lucy must be out of her mind. You're to have hot water every twenty minutes."

"Just hot water?" said Susan.

"Yes, of course," said Charlotte, kicking the bed

again on her return journey, "you've got a high temperature you know."

"How high?" said Susan uneasily, wondering if *she* were about to find herself at death's door.

"The patient isn't supposed to ask questions like that," said Charlotte. "Well, I suppose I'd better put your pillows right and make them comfortable."

"They *are* comfortable," said Susan.

"Well, I'll put them right just the same," said Charlotte. She pushed Susan off her pillows in an extremely rough way, beat them up unmercifully, and left them exactly as Susan didn't want them. "Oh, and you've to get medicine too," she said to her suffering patient. "Every four hours."

"Charlotte," said Susan, "why do you keep shouting at me?"

"I'm not shouting," shouted Charlotte. "Open your mouth and take this."

"Just like that?" said Susan, aghast. "That huge pill? It would choke me."

"Oh, that's right," said Charlotte, "Aunt Lucy said to crush it." She looked about her for some heavy instrument with which to crush it, but finding nothing more suitable than Susan's hairbrush began to bang it with that. Not surprisingly, when she did hit it, which wasn't for some time, the powder flew in all directions.

At each bang Susan winced. When the pill had

finally disintegrated and Charlotte was on her knees on the floor trying to salvage it, Susan said weakly, "You're not going to give me that, are you?"

"Yes, why not?" said Charlotte. "The floor's clean. More or less," she added, picking a little speck of fluff out of the white powder.

"When Mother gives me a pill that has to be crushed," said Susan, trying again, "she puts it in a clean envelope or piece of paper and rolls it with the rolling-pin."

"What a good idea," said Charlotte. "I'll go and do that, and get some fresh air at the same time. Away from these germs." She went out, kicking the bed as she passed.

What a blessed stillness settled over the room. Susan quickly rearranged her pillows and thankfully laid her throbbing head on their coolness. She was still shivering and burning both at once, which was extremely unpleasant. A fresh hot-water bottle would be very nice, but that meant involving Charlotte, and Susan didn't want— didn't want to *bother* Charlotte just at the moment. Besides, she felt she could sleep now, she had had such a rotten night. How blissful it was just to drift off to sleep!

She started awake with Charlotte kicking the bed. "You can't go to sleep just now," shouted Charlotte severely. "Here's your medicine." She proffered a teaspoon with the white powder in it.

"I can't take it like *that*," said Susan, "if it's M. and B. You put it in sugar or powdered glucose and give me a drink to wash it down."

Charlotte looked at her as if she'd like to give it to her in powdered arsenic. "Have I got to go away downstairs again to get you sugar?" she demanded. "Are you a baby?"

"Well, how would you like it as it is?" said Susan. "Hasn't Uncle Charles given M. and B. to you in glucose?"

"I've never had M. and B.," said Charlotte. "I'm never ill. Touch wood!" She leant over Susan to touch wood and kicked the bed. "Oh, well, I suppose I'd better get you some sugar—I shouldn't think we'd have any glucose unless Daddy's had a sample sent him." She went to the door, kicking the bed as she passed.

Susan would gladly have thrown something at her, but she had nothing suitable to hand, nor sufficient energy, for that matter. "You forgot your mask this time," she said spitefully.

"Oh, bother," cried Charlotte, clapping her hand to her mouth. She ran from the room, banging the door.

However, she was very soon back, and Susan took her medicine, and Charlotte jerked one of her pillows away from her and told her she would be down in the schoolroom if Susan wanted her —Susan had only to call. Susan thought that she would be pretty well out of her senses before she called that clumsy maniac once she had got rid of her, but she said yes, Charlotte, thank you, and the minute Charlotte had left the room she rearranged her pillows and settled down to sleep. But the light from the little window that looked on to Tollgate Road and the empty house next door worried her, so she got up and rather totteringly went to it and drew the curtains. She noticed the thermometer lying where Aunt Lucy had left it on the dressing-table, so she thought that she might as well take her temperature and see how ill she really was. It was probably about a hundred and five by now, thanks to Charlotte; but even after she had sucked the thermometer for quite some time, it only registered a hundred and one.

"I don't expect it's working," she thought, and laid it on the hot-water bottle. Then at first she couldn't read it because the mercury had shot right to the top or the end or whatever you called it. "Well, that shows it's not working properly," she thought, "because this bottle is cold. I wish I'd asked Charlotte to fill it. I'll certainly not sleep, because my feet are cold." She wondered for a little if cold feet or Charlotte were the greater evil, but decided at last that cold feet were, because that might make her chill worse and it was quite bad enough—even if her temperature was only a hundred and one, it *felt* like a hundred and five.

"Charlotte!" she called. "Charlotte!"

Charlotte flung open the door. "What *is* it?" she said.

Susan quailed. "Please, Charlotte, could you fill my bottle for me, please?" she begged humbly, "my feet are a wee bit cold."

"'A wee bit cold!'" Charlotte muttered and kicked the bed. "Where *is* the bottle?" she said, and pulled out all the blankets at the foot of the bed. She fumbled in between the wrong ones several times, getting more and more irritated.

"It's between the sheets" murmured Susan. "If you find the sheets——"

Charlotte found the sheets by laying Susan bare to the waist with the blankets over her face. "Oh, here it is," said Charlotte, putting a cold hand on Susan's leg by mistake. She then bundled the blankets untidily in at the foot, kicked the bed and went off to fill the bottle.

"Oh, I'll take it," said Susan quickly when she brought it back.

"No, no," said Charlotte, "I'll pop it in for you. Do the job properly, you know." She did it properly; pulled back the blankets again and thrust the bottle at Susan's naked feet. Susan's yell might have been heard at the other end of the village—Charlotte had forgotten to put the cover on the bottle.

"Well, you said your feet were a wee bit cold," she said, when this had been rectified. "And here's your hot water—it's a little early but you might as well have it now and save me a trot. I brought it up with me."

Feeling guilty, Susan took the water. "Thank you, Charlotte," she said, sipping it and thinking how dull it was. "Charlotte," she said, "why don't you sit down and do a little sketching or reading or something?"

"Well, I don't want to sit in this germ-laden atmosphere," said Charlotte, jerking open the curtains. "And the last time I went down to the schoolroom I had no sooner got settled than you called me."

"I'm awfully sorry, Charlotte," said Susan. "Honestly, I won't call you again."

"Oh, you must call me if you want anything," said Charlotte. "I'm supposed to be nursing you, aren't I?"

"Yes, of course," said Susan. "Thanks awfully, but honestly I won't want anything."

Only peace—she thought, as Charlotte kicked the bed and went out. And for fifteen blessed minutes she had it. She shivered and burned, her feet were cold, her head ached, but it was bliss all the same. She got out of bed and shut the curtains and settled down in bed again. "*Now* I will get to sleep," she said and closed her eyes.

She was wakened by Charlotte kicking the bed. "Here's your hot water," Charlotte said . . .

When Midge and Bill came in, glowing and red-cheeked from their tobogganing, they found Susan almost prostrate.

"Midge," she said quietly, glancing at the door, "have you ever heard of people actually dying from a chill?"

Midge said cheerfully, "Oh, I think there would have to be complications—like pneumonia, you know, first."

"Well, how do you get pneumonia?" said Susan. "If the blankets were pulled off you—by mistake I mean—would you get pneumonia?"

Midge began to giggle. "Did she pull the blankets off you, Susie?" she said.

Bill began to giggle too. "What else did she do Susie? We told you, didn't we?"

"Oh, what *didn't* she do!" said Susan weakly, thankfully giving up all ideas of loyalty to Charlotte. "She kicked the bed and burned my legs and pulled the bed to bits—*look* at it—she tried to make me swallow M. and B. tablets *whole* and—Midge, why d'you think she kept shouting at me?"

"Oh, she always does that when you're ill," said Midge, "as if you were deaf or a foreigner. It kills you when you've got a sore head."

Susan was just going to describe a little of what she had suffered at Charlotte's hands, when Charlotte came in. When Midge and Bill saw her mask, however, they began to shriek with laughter. Even Susan eventually realised that it was just possible that there might be a funny side to her recent sufferings and began to giggle rather feebly. "Take off that mask, you idiot," said Midge, "you know quite well that Susie's not infectious."

"I don't know about infectious," said Charlotte rather shamefacedly, stuffing her home-made mask into her pocket, "but she's jolly cantankerous, I can tell you."

"Well, of course," said Midge, "all your patients won't be as bad as Susie."

"All my patients?" interrupted Charlotte. "*All* my patients! I never want to *see* another patient. And that goes for you too, Susan, my love," she said, and kicking the bed she left the room.

CHAPTER EIGHT

THE EMPTY HOUSE NEXT DOOR

"Now I've done it," thought Susan, when the others, still giggling, had gone down to lunch. "Now I've completely ruined her life. It's a great pity that I can't mind my own business. But on the other hand," she thought, "no one could call Charlotte any great loss to nursing. In fact," she thought more confidently, "I've probably saved countless lives and really ought to have a medal."

This idea sent a pleasant glow through her and she lay happily imagining herself having a medal pinned on her chest, although she couldn't quite work out who was pinning it—Royal Humane Society, she supposed. "No, really," she thought, "I haven't done so badly over Charlotte. It didn't quite work out the way I meant, but after all Aunt Lucy *was* right, and Charlotte will probably end up by being grateful too, although it's a pity about the Latin. . . ."

But now, what about Midge? Aunt Lucy certainly wasn't right about Midge, because it would be absolutely awful if Midge left St. Ronan's just when Susan *was* going. Not that that would matter really, of course, if it was best for Midge, but Susan was sure it wasn't best for Midge. Surely you had to be mad on dancing before making it your career? And Midge didn't seem to be exactly mad on it. Of course, Susan admitted, Midge was lazy, and would probably have to be pushed a wee bit into any career other than sitting with her feet up reading books all day. But dancing—at this potty school too—no, no, something would have to be done about that. It was a very great pity that Miss Pershore couldn't mind her own business instead of interfering in people's lives and recommending schools right and left. It would be a very good thing if Aunt Lucy stopped listening to Miss Pershore's advice. Why couldn't they quarrel? Or be made to quarrel? But Susan didn't at all see how she could engineer that because she hadn't the least idea what two grown women would be likely to quarrel about. If only Aunt Lucy didn't *admire* Miss Pershore so much!

Midge came in with a glass of hot milk.

"It's a bit late for elevenses, isn't it?" said Susan.

"This is your dinner," said Midge.

"My dinner!" said Susan. "Is that all I've to get for dinner?"

"I'm afraid so," said Midge apologetically. "It's your temperature, you see. But Daddy will be up to have a look at you when he's had his coffee, and p'raps you'll be able to have something for tea."

"I'll be dead by tea-time," said Susan gloomily, sipping her milk. "Although I must say," she added, "I don't exactly feel hungry, only weak. From lack of food, I should think. Can you stay and talk to me for a little?"

"Oh, yes," said Midge. "We're going back to the golf-course later; you don't mind, do you? But Aunt Lucy seemed to think you'd want to sleep anyway."

"Of course I don't mind. As long as the snow doesn't disappear before I'm better. . . . Is Charlotte going with you?"

"Oh, yes," grinned Midge. "Charlotte formally renounced all idea of becoming a nurse at lunch-time. Aunt Lucy's going to look after you."

"In that case," said Susan thankfully, "I probably will sleep. Midge," she went on after a little, "you don't happen to know if Miss Pershore leads a double life, do you?"

Midge looked a little startled. "She hasn't confided in me if she does," she said. "But I shouldn't think it's very likely, should you?"

"No," sighed Susan. "It's a pity all the same because what I thought was, that Aunt Lucy wouldn't be so ready to listen to her recommendations—about schools and that—if she were really a jewel thief in disguise. Or something."

Midge thought over this startling observation. "Well," she said, "she still would if Miss Plum's disguise was good enough."

"So she would," said Susan, disgusted. "We'd have to unmask her."

Midge wondered how they were going to unmask something that didn't exist, and decided that Susan would recover from those fantastic ideas when her temperature went down. Bill came in to see if Midge was ready and to ask Susan if Chang was with her. Susan said he wasn't, and then Uncle Charles came to pay a professional visit: the toboggan party departed, and Susan settled down for a peaceful afternoon. . . .

When she awakened she felt wonderfully better, and the red winter sun was setting. There had been no thaw, she noticed with pleasure, and the little bit of Tollgate Road that she could see out of the side window still looked like a Christmas card—the kind Aunt Lucy didn't like. Even the empty house next door, of which she got an excellent view of the gable and a very dilapidated side-door, and a big window inadequately boarded up, even the empty house looked enchanted. . . . Susan suddenly sat up in bed— apparently the house *was* enchanted, for between the boards in the window appeared the little smoky face of Chang! He struggled half-through the opening, looked round, squawked piteously

—not that Susan could hear him, but she could see his poor little mouth opening—struggled back the way he had come and disappeared.

"What a chump he is," thought Susan, "he can't get out. Why doesn't he come out the way he went in? But what a good thing I saw him! He might not be able to get out on his own and we should never have known where to look for him, although I must say we should probably have heard him. When the others come home I'll tell them."

But apparently the others were home, for the door opened quietly and Bill put his head inside the room.

"Oh, hallo, Susan," he said, when he saw that she was awake. He came in, and with elaborate nonchalance looked about the room and twitched Susan's eiderdown.

"If you're looking for Chang," said Susan, "I know where he is."

Bill's worried, handsome little face broke into a wide grin of relief. "Oh, gosh, Susan, do you? Where?" he said.

"In the empty house next door," said Susan. "I've just seen the silly chump at that window."

"Oh, what a relief!" said Bill, sighing gustily. "I've been looking for him all afternoon. He didn't come in for his dinner, and that was rather worrying. I thought he must be up here with you, but he wasn't, and I came up just now for another look—you know the way you keep on looking in a place you've looked before just in the *hope*——"

"Then you weren't up at the golf-course sledging this afternoon?" said Susan.

"No," said Bill.

"Because you were looking for Chang?"

"Well," said Bill, a little embarrassed, "we didn't want to have to tell you that Chang was lost and send your temperature up again."

"Bill!" said Susan, and gulped, "Bill—oh, Bill I *wish* I could buy you an electric train!"

"Gosh, I wish you could!" said Bill. "However——" he said. "I'd better go and see if I can rescue that fool of a cat before it gets dark. If I can't get into the house I'll have to put a ladder up against that window and try to entice him out. I've got a nice pungent bit of haddock downstairs that might do it."

"Haddock!" said Susan. "Chang likes halibut and sole——"

"He hasn't had any dinner," said Bill, "so he may settle for haddock. Be seeing you!"

Susan thought, as soon as he had gone, "*Somehow* I'll get him an electric train, if it kills me." Yes, but how? Susan lay and devised schemes. Even with all her Christmas money she only had thirty shillings, and some of that was supposed to last until she went to St. Ronan's. Of course, she had two book tokens for seven-and-six—

maybe Charlotte or Midge would give her cash for them—maybe. "If I were really noble," she thought, "I'd sell my camera and my watch." The thought of this was such agony to her that it was with tremendous relief that she realised that she hadn't an idea of how to sell a camera and watch. "I'll think of something else. Of course if we unmasked Miss Plum, Aunt Lucy would probably tear the puppets limb from limb—but that would be a pity too, because they're nice. And of course there's that business of there being nothing to unmask—bother, I'd forgotten. I wonder if Bill could give a show? He's awfully clever with his hands—I could help him, not that *I'm* clever with my hands, goodness knows, but I could work the curtains. . . . And we would charge for admission, of course."

She had got to a very advanced stage in her day-dream by the time that Bill came back triumphantly bearing the truant Chang.

"I discovered where he got in," said Bill. "There are some loose boards in one of the basement windows at the back. I went in and waved the haddock and old Chang charged at me like a baby tank.. Was he glad to see that haddock!"

Chang leapt out of Bill's arms on to Susan's bed. He kneaded at her eiderdown for a little until Susan pushed him away, then he settled down beside her, purring madly.

"What was it like in there?" said Susan.

"Oh—spooky—and dark—and great piles of furniture all over the place. And rats," said Bill, in a sepulchral voice.

Susan gave a little shriek. "Did you *see* any?" she said.

"'Course I didn't, it was dark I tell you," said Bill. "I heard them. I'll nail up those boards to-morrow."

Bill didn't nail up the boards; he didn't remember; if he had, a lot of things would have turned out very differently for Susan and the Carmichaels.

Susan was still shuddering over the rats, both on her own account and on Chang's, when Midge and Charlotte came in, ravenously hungry and full of plans to go back to the golf-course when the moon came up. Aunt Lucy wasn't much struck with this scheme. She hadn't an idea when the moon would be up, but she was pretty certain that it would be too late for Midge and Bill and, probably, for Charlotte too. But then it turned out that some of the grown-ups were going to take their cars and shine the headlights on the slope, after tea, and Aunt Lucy said she thought they must be mad, their cars would stick in the snow, and anyway Bill wasn't to go.

So Bill came up to Susan's room so that they could console each other. "I've brought the puppets up," he said. "You can watch and see how I'm getting on. Oh, and here's the evening paper if you want to have a look at it. There's another bit about smuggling watches and a smashing bit about a jewel robbery. Look, there!"

"'WEST-END JEWEL GANG STRIKE AGAIN,'" read Susan. "West End! What's the good of that to Joe?"

"I know," said Bill. "I wish we could move. Well, if you've finished reading that bit, what about helping me with those puppets?"

"Oh, yes," said Susan. Bill took the puppets out of their box and hung them up on the light switches and other convenient places

Bill sat on the floor and looked at them. There were two clowns, and a cowboy and a Dutch girl. "How do we organise that party into a show?" said Bill.

"Well, the clowns are easy," said Susan, "they do something together—a comic boxing-match, maybe. Then the Dutch girl can do a dance while you sing."

"I'm not going to *sing*," said Bill, affronted.

"Why not?" said Susan. "You sang at the carol-singing."

"That was different," said Bill, "it was dark. Besides, it was for a good cause."

"Well, you'll be behind a screen this time. And I can't think of a better cause than your electric train."

Bill agreed about that, and promised to think

about singing, only he didn't know any Dutch songs. Susan said that she did and would teach him one; and Bill thought that he could rig up a windmill with sails that really turned, with his meccano and the little engine that the girls had given him, and began to get quite enthusiastic.

"When shall we give this show?" he said. "We'll need a few days to practise."

"What about Hogmanay?" said Susan. "That's a nice cheery evening to have a show. Will Aunt Lucy and Uncle Charles come, d'you think, and d'you know any rich grown-ups who would come?"

"Well, the Plum," said Bill, "she's rich. But then she'd be dreadfully critical. . . . But of course she'd be interested too, seeing they're her puppets. Yes, I think she'd come."

"We'll charge her half a crown," said Susan.

Bill looked a little alarmed. "Well," he said, "if you think it's worth it——"

Then they got busy working out the details of the puppets' dances and trying out records on the old gramophone from the schoolroom.

Suddenly Susan, who had apparently been doing some mental arithmetic, said, "Bill, even if they all pay half a crown, which isn't very likely, that only comes to twelve-and-six. It'll be *years* before we collect enough to buy one truck, far less a whole railway."

"I'm trying not to think of that," said Bill.

"But we must think of that," said Susan. "I wish we could sell the puppets for a large sum."

"Nobody in their senses would buy them for a large sum," said Bill.

"Oh, I would," said Susan.

Bill looked at her speculatively. "How much?" he said.

"Well," said Susan, "I've only got thirty shillings, I'm afraid—but we could do better than that. Couldn't we put a notice in the toyshop window? There are masses of notices in that window—I saw them when we walked down the village the other day—fur coats, sewing-machines and pretty kittens wanting a good home. Midge read them all."

"She always does," said Bill. "She's always expecting to find something interesting."

"Puppets would be interesting," said Susan.

Bill made sceptical noises.

"And what d'you imagine Aunt Lucy's going to say if—I say if, mind you—if any customer comes to the door enquiring about the puppets for sale?"

"Imph-huh," Susan agreed, "it would be a wee bit awkward."

"'A *wee* bit awkward'!" said Bill.

The door opened and Aunt Lucy came in. "Bill, your father will be late for supper and I have it all ready just to pop in the oven—would you like to come up to the golf-course with me for an hour, if Susan won't be lonely?"

"Oh, would I ?" said Bill. He hastily packed up the puppets and took them to the schoolroom. Then he came back and stuck his head round the door. "Will you be lonely, Susie?" he inquired politely.

Susan laughed. "Away you go," she said.

When Bill and Aunt Lucy had gone Susan lay brooding. If *only* they could sell the puppets for eight pounds without hurting Aunt Lucy's feelings! If the puppets were lost, that wouldn't hurt her feelings. . . . But a large-ish box of four puppets wasn't a thing you could lose very easily. . . . But supposing they were *stolen*? Aunt Lucy wouldn't keep wondering where they had gone if they were stolen—Susan threw back her bed-clothes, got into her dressing-gown and bedroom slippers and, rather tottery, hurried to the school-room. Quite recklessly she pulled things out of cupboards and drawers and hurled them on the floor: she tipped over a small bookcase. Then she hurried down to Charlotte's room and did the same there. She flung wide the window, and she was just admiring this artistic touch when she heard the family arriving home, stamping the snow off their boots at the back door and laughing.

"Help!" thought Susan. "The puppets! Oh, help, oh, help——" She ran back to the school-room and grabbed the box of puppets. She looked round her wildly. She heard someone call out and begin to run upstairs as she darted back to her own room. Tearing off her dressing-gown she leapt into bed. Thrusting the box of puppets down at her feet and bunching up the eiderdown a bit to hide the outline, she shut her eyes and lay trembling.

Midge came into the room crying, "Oh, *Susie*, it was lovely! What a shame you——"

"M-m-m-m?" muttered Susan, stirring in the bed and half-opening her eyes.

"Oh, and now I've wakened you, I *am* sorry," said Midge.

"That's all ri'," mumbled Susan. "I am awake."

"Honestly, I can't tell you how wonderful it was in the dark!" said Midge. "There was a moon and the car headlights and it's freezing again, you know, so it was all crispy and sparkly, and somehow it was much, *much* more thrilling in the dark, wasn't it, Aunt Lucy?"

Aunt Lucy had just come in to inquire after Susan.

"Oh, Susie's all right," Midge assured her "sleeping like a baby when I came in."

"Well, look, darling, I'll just——" Aunt Lucy was beginning when there was a sudden terrible scream.

Midge and Aunt Lucy ran to the door, and they heard Charlotte calling, "Aunt *Lucy*! Come quickly!" Midge and Aunt Lucy hurried away, and Susan lay in bed, smirking happily.

It wasn't long before they were back, and Charlotte too. Midge was beside herself with excitement. "And to think of Susan lying there sleeping! She might have been murdered in her bed!"

"*Midge!*" exclaimed Susan sitting up and acting very naturally, she considered. "What are you talking about?"

"We've had a burglar, that's what," said Midge, her eyes sparkling. "Charlotte's room is a *shambles* and the window's been left open banging against the wall—I expect that's how he got away."

There was another yell of excitement in the distance. "Aunt Lucy! Come and see the schoolroom! He's been here too—my puppets are gone!" called Bill. Midge darted away to examine this fresh cause for excitement, followed by the others.

In a little while they came back into Susan's room, all talking at once, Bill's voice rising above the rest. "I'll go and telephone my friend Joe now, shall I, Aunt Lucy?" he shouted. "He'll be jolly glad of a little bit of trouble in this dead-and-alive place, I should think. Shall I phone him now, Aunt Lucy?"

"Oh, be quiet, all of you," said Aunt Lucy, looking harassed. When the noise had more or less subsided she glanced over at Susan. "Didn't you hear anything?" she said.

Midge saved Susan the necessity of replying. "Susan was sleeping when I came in," she said.

"Has nothing else been taken that you know of?" said Aunt Lucy. "It seems so odd only taking a box of puppets."

"Only a box of puppets!" said Bill with some heat. "Shall I phone Joe now, Aunt Lucy? We don't want to waste a minute. I'll go and phone now, shall I?"

"Bill, do stop nagging," said Aunt Lucy. "I don't want you to telephone until I've spoken to your father. Midge, go and ask Miss Bracken how many more patients there are waiting and how long she thinks he'll be."

Midge went off, and Bill grumbled away to himself that every minute was precious, didn't they realise that? And the burglar was probably out of the country by this time. When Midge came back and reported that there were only three more patients, but that one of them was Miss Fairweather, a notoriously lengthy recounter of symptoms, the whole family groaned, and Aunt Lucy said distractedly, "We'll *never* get our supper to-night. Bill, perhaps you ought to go down and get started, I'll come with you—no, Charlotte you go. I'll get Susan ready for the night—Susan d'you think you could sit by the fire a moment while I make your bed?"

Susan stared at her, aghast. "Make my bed!" she gasped at last.

"Yes!" said Aunt Lucy, smiling a little. "It's not so terribly unusual, is it?"

"Oh, Aunt Lucy, it doesn't need making," said Susan earnestly, "honestly it doesn't."

"Nonsense," said Aunt Lucy.

"You go and give Bill his supper," said Susan, getting desperate, "and Midge will give me a hand."

Aunt Lucy's answer to this was to twitch off the eiderdown. "Come on, get up and don't blether," she said. "You children would argue the hind legs off a——" She stopped, staring at the tell-tale square shape outlined under the bed-clothes.

Then she stared at Susan. Susan began to blush. And when Susan blushed, it seemed to start at her toes and work its way up until she was one vast glow of crimson.

"Susan!" said Aunt Lucy reproachfully, and pulled back the blankets. "Oh, Susan, *really*," she said. "You deserve a good spanking, upsetting us all like this. But I'm so thankful that it wasn't a real burglar that I can't be too cross with you. The idea of a burglar being in the *house* and touching our things made me feel sick. I suppose this was in aid of Joe's promotion too?" She didn't wait for an answer, which was lucky, Susan felt. "Only what Charlotte's going to say when she hears that she has you to thank for all that mess!"

Charlotte, when she heard, said that Susan could jolly well clean it up. But Aunt Lucy wouldn't allow that either because of Susan catching more cold and her temperature going up again; but when Bill heard the whole story from Susan, he actually offered to clean up the mess himself, a fact which puzzled Aunt Lucy for days whenever she thought of it. . . .

Susan was rather disgusted to discover next morning that Uncle Charles wasn't going to let her get up yet.

"But I'm perfectly well now, Uncle Charles," she said. "I haven't a temperature."

"You have a temperature all right; you'd be in a bad way if you hadn't," said Uncle Charles; "but it's normal."

"There you are then," said Susan. "I'm better."

"Yes, I know," said Uncle Charles. "Perhaps we'll get you up this afternoon."

So Susan had to be patient. It was very tiresome, because now she felt perfectly well and longed to be up; and to make matters worse, Charlotte came in with the news that the lake in the park was bearing, that the snow had been swept off it, and everybody was skating. However, Miss Pershore, back from Paris, called in to see her, and gave her some luscious chocolates.

Then Bill brought in the puppets and they prac-
tised a little, for Bill had tossed up with Midge
for the skates they shared and had lost; and she
had plenty to read, and she could watch the little
that was going on in Tollgate Road. There even
seemed to be some activity in the empty house
next door, for a green and white Ivor Williams
van drove up and two men carefully carried a
small chest of drawers from the house to the van.
Later in the morning an Ivor Williams van again
arrived and two men carefully carried a small
chest of drawers from the van to the house.
"Always something going on," said Susan to
herself. But when early in the afternoon, a van
again drove up and two men carried out what
looked to Susan the identical chest of drawers,
she got rather bored with vans and furniture and
decided that Ivor Williams were mad. If she had
been watching out of the side window next
morning she would have seen the same little
chest of drawers go out again from the house next
door and surely her "inflamed imagination"
would have made something of that; but at
that time next morning Susan was happily
sliding round the lake in the park. It was Bill's
turn for the skates, and he was hurtling round
the pond in a very dramatic way. Midge and
Susan had to content themselves with sliding,
but Charlotte had promised to lend Susan her
skates later on, their feet being the same size.

Susan had never skated before, but she was longing to try—it looked so graceful and so easy. At lunch-time Aunt Lucy wondered whether she ought, after being in bed, but Uncle Charles seemed to think that it would be all right if she didn't get overheated and so get another chill.

"Overheated!" thought Susan later, lying on her back on the ice for the twentieth time, "I shall die of exposure. And be glad to——"

Midge, in a curious doubled-up position, tottered towards her. "Come on, Susie," she said. "I'll help you up."

"Midge," said Susan, "if I get up on these ankles of mine again they'll break in two. I can't *tell* you what agony I'm in."

"Well, I know," said Midge. "But that goes off after a bit. Come on, get up."

Susan got up and Midge went down. This see-saw effect might have gone on long enough, but one of the Vernon boys came to the rescue and got them both on their feet, clinging together, giggling helplessly. Eventually they staggered off again, clutching each other by the hand. "You must have more confidence, Susan," said Midge. "And *glide*, don't tittup along like a hen. Strike out boldly. Look at Bill—well you can't just now when he's up at the golf-course, but you know what I mean—he started skating when I did, and he charges round like an ice-hockey player and can do figure threes and the Dutch Roll and—oh, *Susan*!"

Susan had struck out boldly—and her feet had struck out too, and she was in her accustomed recumbent position on the ice. "Don't you think," she said, getting on to her hands and knees and crawling to the edge of the pond "don't you think Charlotte would like her skates now? I don't want to be selfish about them."

"Oh, well," said Midge, "maybe you've done enough for the first day."

"And perhaps it'll thaw in the night!" said Susan hopefully.

It was bliss to get back into ordinary shoes again, although rather peculiar. The feeling gradually came back into her toes, although her ankles, she felt, were ruined for life, and by the time she and Midge got home and found Aunt Lucy in the kitchen baking Scotch pancakes for tea, Susan was enthusiastically acclaiming skating to be the most exhilarating of occupations.

Aunt Lucy handed them hot pancakes, dripping with butter. Susan thought, "Aunt Lucy really is a super aunt," but she felt inclined to revise her opinion when Aunt Lucy wiped her hands in the very middle of hot pancakes and rhapsodies about skating to go and fetch a poem for Susan to read. "Oh, help," thought Susan, "is she going to improve *my* mind?" When Aunt Lucy came back with the poem it turned out to be by no highbrow modern poet, but by Wordsworth, who, everybody knew, was the greatest bore in the poetic line.

"Do I read it *all*?" she said aghast, flipping over the pages of *The Prelude*.

"Well, of course you needn't—unless you want to," said Aunt Lucy, "but there's a nice little bit about skating I thought you'd like. When we were children and lived in Glasgow we used to skate on Lochwinnoch—miles of glorious ice— you don't get the same effect, naturally, on the lake in the park. But you'll like Wordsworth's description—listen——

> ' *And in the frosty season, when the sun*
> *Was set, and visible for many a mile*
> *The cottage windows blazed through twilight*
> *   gloom,*
> *I heeded not their summons: happy time*
> *It was indeed for all of us—for me*
> *It was a time of rapture!   Clear and loud*
> *The village clock tolled six,—I wheeled about,*
> *Proud and exulting like an untired horse*
> *That cares not for his home.   All shod with steel,*
> *We hissed along the polished ice in games*
> *Confederate, imitative of the chase*
> *And woodland pleasures,—the resounding horn,*
> *The pack loud chiming, and the hunted hare.*

S.P.S.

E

> *So through the darkness and the cold we flew,*
> *And not a voice was idle; with the din*
> *Smitten, the precipices rang aloud;*
> *The leafless trees and every icy crag*
> *Tinkled like iron——'"*

Susan did, rather to her surprise, like it, and felt inspired to dash out again after tea, or early next morning, to try again. Only, of course, it would be the turn of Charlotte and Bill to have the skates.

"Where are the others?" said Midge, eating more hot buttered pancakes, "aren't they coming in for tea?"

Aunt Lucy heaved herself away from the kitchen dresser where she had been leaning, reading to the end of the passage about skating.

"They've gone to the Greenwoods' for tea," she said. "Charlotte phoned a little while ago. Oh, and by the way, Susan, Chang's missing."

"Ugh, not again," said Susan. "He'll be next door, I expect, the chump."

"Probably he's fascinated by all those rats," said Midge.

"Don't!" Susan shuddered. "They'll attack him. I'll have to go in and rescue him—after tea, of course. I wish Bill were here."

"I'll come with you," said Midge.

That would always be something, thought Susan.

But all the same, it would be better if Bill came home and went after Chang. Or if Chang came home . . .

But Chang didn't come home. Susan stood gazing up at the big side-window of the house next door and called him and made encouraging noises, and even roundly abused him, but Chang didn't appear.

"Why don't you let him stay there for a bit?" said Midge. "It wouldn't hurt him. Might teach him a lesson."

"But supposing the rats ate him?" said Susan, her dark eyes wide.

"I don't think that's very likely," said Midge. "Besides, I don't believe there are any rats there. They wouldn't be good for the furniture. I expect Ivor Williams put traps down, or poison."

"Traps! Poison!" cried Susan. "Come *on*!"

Midge, who wasn't particularly keen on this expedition herself, felt she had only herself to blame for putting ideas into Susan's head, so she went off to fetch torches. She led Susan to a hole in the fence between the two gardens through which they squeezed, and across the deep crisp snow to the back of the house next door. They soon found the window with the loose boards.

"There it is," said Susan. "Carry on, Midge."

"After you," said Midge politely.

Susan gave her a rather hurt look, sighed, and

reluctantly began to climb in the window. "I don't think I can get in," she said thankfully.

"Of course you can," said Midge, "I'll give you a push. And do hurry up because it's getting dark now."

Susan quite realised that this expedition, bad as it was, would be a thousand times worse in pitch darkness. She squeezed through the opening. She found herself in a sort of cellar, which was quite empty—of rats or anything else. So she took courage a little from this and whispered to Midge, "Okay, I'm in. Come on!" and Midge climbed in after her.

"Well," said Midge, "call him."

"Chang! Chang! Chang!" called Susan obediently.

"Chee-chee-chee," said Midge. "Puss, puss, puss!"

"He doesn't really answer to 'puss,'" said Susan, "he likes his name better."

"He's jolly lucky I'm calling him at all," said Midge severely. "Well, he isn't exactly rushing to welcome us, so we'd better go upstairs and look for him."

"Yes," said Susan. "Don't make a noise."

"Why not?" said Midge. "In case we disturb the dear little rats?"

"In case any of the furniture men hear us," said Susan feebly.

"Is that likely?" said Midge. "They've all gone

home by this time—and anyway they're hardly ever here, only to move some stuff occasionally."

"I saw two yesterday," said Susan, very much wishing they were there to-day. She'd rather be caught trespassing by a furniture man than— "What's that?" she gasped, clutching Midge.

Midge released herself. "*I* didn't hear anything," she said. "Do come on, Susan, before you start me gibbering too."

They went cautiously up the stone stairs to the ground floor calling, "Chang, Chang!" softly, and shining their torches round the rooms filled with unknown shapes, sheeted and sinister. But no little purring cat came running to meet them. It was very cold and the rooms smelt musty. The corner of a dust-sheet moved in a draught, and Susan grabbed Midge's arm again.

"Something moved!" she whispered, "over there in the corner!"

"Ouch, *Susan*, my arm!" said Midge. "Do remember my sensitive skin. I bruise very easily. And if you're imagining the house is haunted, you needn't."

"Well, it's an old house," objected Susan. "It might easily be."

"Nonsense!" said Midge. "Come along. We'd better go upstairs, and cheer up, for goodness' sake. Just imagine we're playing hide-and-seek in the dark."

Susan didn't think that her imagination was

as good as all that, but the idea was a help, so she crept upstairs after Midge. There was more furniture upstairs, but still no Chang.

"Of course you know," said Midge, "Chang might not *be* here at all."

"Well," said Susan crossly, "after all we've gone through for him!"

"Just because he was here yesterday," said Midge, ignoring Susan's unreasonable outburst, "doesn't mean he must be here to-day. But I suppose we'd better go upstairs and make sure. Perhaps he's having a quiet snooze somewhere."

Susan didn't think that she could stand much more, but she certainly didn't want to be left alone there while Midge went upstairs, so she followed her to the top floor. The rooms were dusty here and empty, except that when they shone their torches into the back room on the left of the stairs, a small, dainty chest of drawers stood in the middle of the floor.

"Well, I'm bothered!" said Susan. "That's the chest I saw those men carrying in and out yesterday! I thought at the time they must be potty."

"What *are* you talking about?" said Midge.

"Well," said Susan, "when I was in bed—you know you get a good view of this house from the side window in our bedroom—I watched two men carrying this chest of drawers out to a van. About a couple of hours later they carried it in again. And after dinner they carried it out *again*."

"How do you know it's the same chest of drawers?" said Midge.

"Well, I don't *know*," said Susan. "It looks like it. It seemed potty to me, carrying the same chest in and out all day."

"They *could*—" Midge worked it out—"they could have taken the chest of drawers somewhere, found they had made a mistake and brought it back. And then discover that they were right in the first place and take it out again."

"But the chest's *here*," said Susan, waving her torch at it. "So they must have brought it back again. Potty." She went nearer to the chest. She rubbed her hand over its beautiful top, bright from the loving care of many years' polishing. "No dust, you see," she said, and then stopped short, her hand in mid-air, her torch directed on the chest. "Listen!" she said. "Come over here and listen."

Midge obligingly drew near and listened. "What am I listening for?" she said, after a little.

Susan said, "Can't you hear a faint tick-tick-tick?"

Midge put her head down towards the chest of drawers and listened again. "Yes," she said, "I believe I can. Coming from the chest."

Once more she found her arm gripped in Susan's

vice-like grasp. "Come back, Midge! Come back!" gasped Susan.

"Well, for goodness' sake, Susie," said Midge, "what is it now?"

"It's a bomb, that's what," said Susan, still backing towards the door, and trying to pull Midge after her.

Midge shook her arm loose. "Oh, come now, Susie," she said soothingly. "Not bombs as well! I mean, you can have rats and ghosts *or* bombs, but not them all."

"But what else could it be?" said Susan. "That's the one thing I know about bombs. They tick."

"So do watches," said Midge.

Susan's mouth dropped open and she gaped at Midge. "Watches!" she said. "Watches!" and to Midge's amazement she darted to the chest of drawers and began opening drawer after drawer. "Ugh!" she exclaimed. "Empty!"

Midge gazed at her curiously. "What did you expect to find?" she said.

"Watches," said Susan. Then she gave a little shamefaced laugh and said, "Ugh, I must be daft, but somehow when you said that watches tick, something seemed to tick in my head and I remembered all those smuggled watches that Bill and I have been reading about in the papers. But, of course, how could they get into this chest of drawers? I'm daft. Come on and let's go home. Chang isn't here."

But by this time Midge's interest, too, was thoroughly aroused. She said slowly, "Well, I wouldn't know how they'd get here and all the drawers are certainly empty, but there *is* a ticking sound," and she bent her head again towards the chest of drawers and listened.

"It's the death-watch beetle," said Susan. "Come on!"

"Susie, hold this torch for me a minute," said Midge. "I'm going to have a look at these drawers. The ticking seems to come from near the bottom."

She pulled open the bottom drawer again.

"Do you see anything funny about that drawer?" she said.

"It's empty," said Susan helpfully.

"I know that, you numskull," said Midge. "But don't you think it's very shallow?"

"Well, yes, I believe it is for a *bottom* drawer," said Susan. "It's always the deepest."

"And now let's see the outside," said Midge, snatching a torch from Susan. "Yes, look," she said when she had shut the drawer, "the bottom one *is* the deepest."

"You don't mean," said Susan, her voice rising to a squeal of excitement, "you don't mean you think that the drawer has a *false bottom*!"

"Could be," said Midge. "I wish I had a ruler to measure."

"Here's my hankie, measure with that," said

Susan, breathing deeply in her excitement. "It's not very clean, I'm afraid."

"You're right!" said Midge. "I'll use my own, thanks! *Do* hold the torch steady, Susie! There you are," she said triumphantly, "the outside of the drawer is that much—a good four inches, I should say—deeper than the inside!"

"Well, come on," said Susan, "for goodness' sake stop measuring and let's see what's inside."

"And supposing—" said Midge—"and supposing it really *is* a bomb and we get blown sky-high?"

"Ugh, we've just got to risk that," said Susan recklessly. All the same she pulled the drawer open very cautiously, and gently began to prise up one of the panels in the bottom with her fingers. "Look," she said, "it comes out quite easily—Midge, *look!*"

Midge shone her torch into the drawer. Gleaming in the torch-light, lying in a soft bed of green baize, were row upon row of watches.

CHAPTER NINE

SUSAN IN DISGRACE

"AND the funny thing was," said Susan, "they were all going!"

"I don't think *that's* the funny thing," said Charlotte, "the funny thing to me is that they were there at all!"

They were all gathered in the schoolroom after supper; and Midge and Susan were recounting their extraordinary discovery in the house next door. Bill had nearly gone mad, and had done a wild dance of glee round the room until peremptorily ordered by his sisters to sit down and shut up.

"Oh, what luck!" he panted. "What luck! Wait till my friend Joe hears about this! He'll round up the gang and be in the C.I.D. and probably made a detective-inspector right away!"

"But what *gang*?" said Charlotte. "What's it all about? I'm in a perfect fog!"

"Me, too!" said Midge.

"Well," said Susan, "it was in the paper. There seems to be a gang at work smuggling thousands of watches into the country."

"It's all perfectly clear to me," said Bill. "Someone, let's call him Mr. X——"

"Oh, *yes*," interrupted Susan, "I love a Mr. X——"

"Well, Mr. X," went on Bill, "smuggles in these watches, takes them to the house next door—in an Ivor Williams van, I shouldn't wonder, then packs them into the chest of drawers. Along comes a van and a couple of men who carry out the chest of drawers—Susan saw them——"

"Yes," said Susan eagerly, "I saw that chest of drawers going out and in—I told you!"

"—They take the watches to the shop, or to the person who is going to sell them, then bring back the chest of drawers for a refill. If anyone looks inside the van, there is only an empty chest of drawers in it, being delivered; and no one is going to pay the slighest attention to a chest of drawers being taken from a furniture store—I've seen men taking furniture in and out of that house hundreds of times and never paid any attention. It was only bad luck for the gang that Susan was lying in bed with nothing to do and noticed that it was the *same* chest of drawers going in and out."

"Then is the gang Ivor Williams?" said Charlotte, more puzzled than ever.

"Gracious no," said Bill, shocked. "Ivor Williams are only being used as a—what's the word? A cover? Yes, a cover."

"Well, you seem to have worked it all out very

successfully, young Bill," said Midge. "But who's Mr. X?"

"How should I know?" said Bill.

"But *I* know *that*," said Susan. "Mr. X is Miss Plum."

There was a stunned silence in the schoolroom while the Carmichaels absorbed this.

Then they began to laugh. They shrieked, they held their aching tummies, Bill rolled on the floor.

"Well, I don't know what the joke is," said Susan, when there was a lull. "It seems perfectly obvious to me."

"But—but—but *Susie*," spluttered Midge, wiping her eyes, "you're not seriously suggesting that Miss Plum is smuggling watches? Why, she's rolling in money!"

"Well, naturally," said Susan. "So would you be if you smuggled twenty thousand pounds' worth of watches into the country from Paris once a fortnight, or however often she goes. I mean, it's sticking out a mile—the day after she returns from Paris the chest of drawers starts going out. I wish very much that we had looked at her petrol tank, Bill."

"But, angel," said Charlotte, slowly realising that Susan was serious, "she's a *friend* of ours!"

"I know. It's dreadful," said Susan. "But I asked you, Midge, if she wasn't leading a double life. I was right, you see. I thought right from the start that she was a queer customer. Blue hair, indeed."

"Oh, Susan, you're hopeless," said Charlotte, getting exasperated. "You can't just sit there and say poor Miss Plum is running a gang of smugglers because she has blue hair."

"You'll land in prison yourself if you go about saying things like that without proof," said Midge severely.

"Bill's friend Joe can get the *proof*," said Susan airily. "That shouldn't be difficult. We won't say anything about it yet. We'll just tell Aunt Lucy."

Charlotte sat up as if she had been shot. "You're not going to Aunt Lucy with this preposterous story!" she said.

"Of course I am," said Susan. "That's the whole point. When Aunt Lucy realises the kind of person Miss Plum is, she won't be so anxious to listen to her advice and send Midge to schools she recommends."

"My poor, demented cousin," began Charlotte, but just then Aunt Lucy's voice was heard calling upstairs that if Susan didn't go to bed soon, she'd be finding herself ill again. And Bill too.

"Susie," whispered Charlotte urgently, "promise, *promise* that you won't breathe a word of this to Aunt Lucy until we've looked into it a little more."

"All right," agreed Susan amiably, "I promise. Only the sooner the better, it seems to me."

"No, *no*," said Charlotte. "It's just a wild guess because the poor woman lives next door to where you saw the watches and goes to Paris. And has blue hair. We haven't a shadow of proof —oh, here am I talking about proof as if there were the faintest possibility of ever getting such proof! It's too ridiculous——"

"Susan! Bill!" called Aunt Lucy.

"Coming, Aunt Lucy," Susan called back. She grinned at Charlotte's worried face. "Cheer up," she whispered, "we'll soon get proof. Come on, Chang!" Chang got up and stretched himself.

"So Chang did turn up then," said Charlotte, who had been too carried away by the fantastic story to remember the cause of it all. "You never told us."

"Ugh, yes," said Susan. "Fast asleep in an arm-chair, if you please. He appeared when we went downstairs again. He loves that house next door."

"Then he's the only one who does," said Charlotte morosely.

Immediately after breakfast next morning Bill shot off to find his friend Joe. He came back sadly disappointed to report that Joe was off-duty, and had gone to see his cousin in Hampstead. Charlotte wanted to skate, but was terrified to let Susan out of her sight. However, Bill promised to look after her, because he wanted Susan anyway for a final rehearsal of the puppet show.

"I hope you're remembering that the show's to-day, by the way," he said. "This is New Year's Eve."

"Well, it can't be this afternoon," said Charlotte. "Aunt Lucy is taking us to the pictures."

"No, after supper," said Bill. "Aunt Lucy said that would be okay. Oh, and Charlotte, I'm afraid we're charging for admission."

"Oh, are you?" said Charlotte. "How much?"

"Would a shilling be too much?" said Bill.

"Yes, it would," said Charlotte.

"All right, sixpence then."

"What's it in aid of?" asked Midge suspiciously.

"The F.B.B.E.T.," said Susan.

"What does all that stand for?" said Charlotte.

"The Fund for Buying Bill an Electric Train," said Susan, "but don't tell Aunt Lucy in case she thinks he's ungrateful."

"Do we let Aunt Lucy think she's contributing to the Red Cross, then?" said Midge.

"Well, no," said Susan. "We thought that we needn't go into details."

"You'll both be senile by the time you've collected enough for an electric train," said Charlotte, rather unfeelingly, Susan thought. "Come on, Midge!"

The skaters departed, and Susan and Bill went

up to the schoolroom. Bill rigged up quite a good stage in one corner with draperies, a clothes-horse and the bed-table. There wasn't a proper curtain, but he fixed the draperies so that they could be pulled back, and after wrecking the whole stage once or twice, Susan eventually mastered this operation to Bill's satisfaction. The two clowns did their boxing-match; the Dutch girl danced while Bill sang and the meccano windmill turned most realistically. Bill had found a hill-billy record for the cowboy to dance to.

"I do think it's going to work up quite nicely," said Bill as they went down to the kitchen to see if Aunt Lucy had provided any elevenses for them. "Not very ambitious, of course, but we don't want to bite off more than we can chew for our first attempt."

Susan didn't take this modest view of it at all; she was tremendously impressed by the show, and gave it as her opinion that it was well worth paying as much as half a crown for admission, and just as good as any professional performance, not that she had seen any, of course, except Miss Plum's.

But when they went upstairs again to the schoolroom after their cocoa and biscuits, disaster met them. Unthinkingly, they had hung one of the clowns within Chang's reach, never expecting him to pay any attention to it. But Chang had more than paid attention to it, he had pulled it down and had had a terrific and enjoyable struggle with it, and now it lay on the floor, a tangled wreck of string and wood and torn clothes, with Chang growling happily over it.

"Oh, Chang, you bad *bad* cat," said Susan, stamping at him.

"Well, I suppose we shouldn't have left it where Chang could get at it," said Bill despairingly, picking up the poor little dangling puppet.

"Let me try to put it right——" said Susan.

"Susan, it's hopeless," said Bill. "We should be here all day untangling those strings; besides, some of them are broken, and the clothes are torn."

"Ugh, I could *howl*," said Susan.

"It spoils the clowns' dance," said Bill, "and it was quite good, I thought. The other clown will have to dance by himself—it's rather dull, but it's all we can do. Come on, let's work out a dance for him."

Susan said slowly, "Bill, d'you think that Miss Plum would *lend* us a puppet?"

"That's not a bad idea," said Bill, brightening. "Let's go and ask her."

"Well, I don't think *I* will," said Susan, "not after all the things I said about her."

"Oh, don't be silly," said Bill. "You didn't mean all that rot, surely?"

Susan allowed herself to follow Bill to Miss

Pershore's beautiful doorway. "Well, of course I meant it," she said.

"Yes," said the elegant maid, still elegant in her morning attire, she thought Madam was in. She was up in her workshop, she thought. Would Miss Susan and Master Bill go up?

Miss Susan and Master Bill went up to Miss Pershore's workshop, the room to the back of the house on the right of the stairs. "Oh, bother," said Bill, looking round the empty room—at least empty of Miss Pershore, "she's not in after all. And I don't suppose we could borrow one without asking."

"Oh, no," said Susan.

"What a pity! There's a clown in that box, not unpacked yet," said Bill wistfully. "I suppose she had them in Paris." He bent down and carefully lifted out the little clown. "Nice, isn't he?" he said.

"'Mm, I like his green hair," said Susan absently. She wasn't looking at the puppet, but gazing down at the green baize on which the puppets were lying. "Green baize rings a bell," she thought, and dropping to her knees she gently turned back the corner of the baize, and slipped her hand in among the puppets in the row below. But her groping fingers found nothing unusual among them.

Bill had unwound the strings of the little clown. "I couldn't borrow this one anyway," he said, "the control is different from my puppets—much more difficult to work. And it's so *heavy*!"

"Heavy, is it?" said Susan curiously. "Let me see!"

Bill handed her the puppet, but Susan somehow fumbled over the strings and the puppet fell with a clatter to the floor.

"Oh, Susie, you clumsy owl," said Bill, and Susan dived to retrieve the little puppet lying grotesquely askew on the floor.

"Oh, help, oh, help!" said Susan. "The strings will be in a hopeless fankle."

"Why don't you talk English?" said Bill. "I suppose you mean tangle?"

Susan was usually quick to defend her Scottish expressions, but this time she didn't even answer. She was on her knees, touching the puppet. "Bill," she said in a terrified voice, "it's broken!"

"It can't be *broken*," said Bill. "It's made of wood."

"Well, but it is," said Susan. "Look—split in the middle of its tummy." She lifted the top half of the puppet and something white fell to the floor. "Oh, *help*," said Susan, "now its inside is coming out—oh, help, we'll never be able to put it together again!" She picked up the white package. "No wonder the puppet was heavy," she said. "This weighs a ton."

"Stuff it back then quick," said Bill, "and I'll try to put the thing together."

But Susan, who never could mind her own business, was unwrapping the tissue paper which covered the package. "Bill, look!" she whispered and held out her hand. On it lay a tiny gold watch.

Bill's eyes nearly started out of his head. "Susie!" he said, "are there any more?"

Susan, with the greatest care, explored the package further. "Hundreds!" she said. "At least——"

"Let's have a look," said Bill.

Susan glanced nervously round the room and especially at the cupboard into which Miss Pershore had disappeared on the night of the party. If she could disappear like that, was there any reason why she couldn't reappear—now?

"Bill," she whispered, "she might catch us! Let's get out of here!"

"Honestly, I can't believe it," said Bill. "You were right after all. Wrap up those watches, quick, and put them back. Look, the puppet fits together perfectly—she has made puppets specially for smuggling!"

"Let's get *out*," said Susan. "I'm terrified!"

Quickly Susan put back the watches. Bill—as best he could—put back the puppet. They went sedately downstairs, sought out the parlourmaid. "Miss Pershore wasn't there," said Bill, "but it doesn't matter, we'll see her later." The maid looked surprised; she let them out.

"Susan," began Bill as they walked down to their own house, "not a word about this!"

But Susan hadn't heard, or if she had heard she didn't pay any attention. She went bursting into the drawing-room, where Midge and Charlotte, just come in from skating, were talking to Aunt Lucy.

"Well, what's the matter with you?" said Midge. "You look——"

"Darling!" said Aunt Lucy, "there's snow on your shoes. You really must remember to wipe your feet or change your shoes before you come charging in."

"I'm awfully sorry, Aunt Lucy," said Susan, "but I hadn't time to change them because I wanted to tell you something."

"Susan, shut up," said Bill, who had followed her into the room.

"Bill," said Aunt Lucy, "don't talk to Susan, or to anybody, like that. And you've got snow on your shoes too—go and wipe your feet!"

Bill reluctantly went, but Susan stayed where she was and the snow off her shoes melted in a dirty little puddle on the carpet. "Oh, help," she said, and went down on her knees and began mopping it up with her handkerchief.

"Never mind it now," said Aunt Lucy. "It'll dry. What's this momentous news that couldn't wait?"

"Susan," said Bill, "shut—be quiet!"

"Susan," said Charlotte, "you're not going to——"

"Susan," said Midge, "don't say one *word*——"

Aunt Lucy gazed in bewilderment from one to another. "What *is* going on?" she said. "Well, come along Susan, tell me!"

"Ugh, well," said Susan uncomfortably, glancing round at her cousins, "maybe I'd better say no more——"

"My dear child," said Aunt Lucy, "I'm eaten up with curiosity by this time. Tell me the worst."

"Yes, well, it's pretty bad——"

"Go *on*, then!"

"Well, Aunt Lucy," Susan began haltingly, "I'm afraid we've discovered that Miss Pershore is a smuggler."

Aunt Lucy's mouth dropped open and she stared at Susan. "What does she smuggle, for goodness' sake?" she said. "My knowledge of smuggling doesn't go much beyond that poem —you know, ' baccy for the merchant, brandy for the clerk——'"

"Well, it's not very much like that poem," said Susan. "It's watches."

"Watches?" said Aunt Lucy.

"Yes," said Susan. "You see," she hurried on, "Midge and I found a chest of drawers with a false bottom in the house next door, and it was full of watches. And you must have read in the papers about all the smuggling of watches that has been going on, there have been cases reported every other day—and it's believed there's quite a gang at work ... and you see ... Miss Pershore ... is one of the gang ..." and Susan's voice tailed off miserably.

"Susan," said Aunt Lucy, and she didn't sound very friendly, "if this is a joke, it's a joke in extremely bad taste."

"It isn't a joke," said Susan in a very small voice.

Then Aunt Lucy exploded. "Then how *dare* you stand there and tell such preposterous lies about one of my friends?" she demanded.

Midge said, "We did find the watches in the chest of drawers, Aunt Lucy."

Aunt Lucy put her hand to her forehead in bewilderment and exasperation. "Midge, really! You too," she said.

"Well, we did, Aunt Lucy," said Midge.

"Well, that's a very extraordinary thing to find," said Aunt Lucy. "But what has it to do with Miss Pershore?"

"You see," said Susan, "we found more watches inside Miss Pershore's puppets, didn't we, Bill?"

Bill, who had been standing by the window, turned and looked at her with an expression which Susan couldn't read. "I don't know what you're talking about," he said.

"*Bill!*" gasped Susan.

And at that moment the drawing-room door opened and a gay voice called out, "May I come in? Really, you people! Leaving your front door open in weather like this!" and Miss Pershore came into the room.

Susan wished she could die. Just drop dead there and then and never have to look Aunt Lucy or Miss Pershore in the face again. For either Bill had gone mad, or she had made some terrible mistake.

She looked at the floor and began to rub with the toe of her shoe the damp spot that the snow had made on the carpet.

"Ellen said you were looking for me, Bill," went on Miss Pershore, probably wondering a little at the general atmosphere of embarrassment.

"Oh, yes, Miss Pershore," Bill began, "I wondered——"

But before he could go on, Aunt Lucy said, "Susan, will you kindly repeat in front of Miss Pershore what you have just been saying?"

"Aunt Lucy!" begged Susan.

"Go on," said Aunt Lucy inexorably.

Susan mumbled, still looking at the floor, "Well, we found a chest of drawers next door full of wee watches, and——" she glanced up at Miss Pershore. Miss Pershore was looking at her with the queerest expression in her light-coloured eyes.

"Go on," said Aunt Lucy.

Susan looked down at the floor again. "And we, that is, *I* thought that you must have something to do with it."

There was a second's silence, then Miss Pershore burst into peals of merry laughter. This was preferable, certainly, to being struck, which was what Susan had rather expected; and after a little Miss Pershore carefully dabbed at her eyes and said, "Oh, Lucia, my dear, you mustn't be cross with her, it's too heavenly a joke—smuggling watches! My poor Susan, if you only *knew* how I tremble coming through the Customs wearing a pair of nylons that I've bought in Paris!"

Aunt Lucy said, "You may be thankful, Susan, that Miss Pershore can find something amusing in this situation, but as I very definitely cannot, I'll be glad if you'll go upstairs out of my sight."

Susan slunk out of the room, and as she went she heard Miss Pershore asking Bill what he wanted her for, and Bill telling her. As Susan went drearily upstairs to the schoolroom, she thought that she could have stood anything— Aunt Lucy's rage, Miss Plum's laughter, the girls' annoyance—anything except Bill's desertion. What did he mean by it? Or was she just going potty herself? Had they really never seen the wee gold watches in the puppet?

In a little while Midge brought her lunch up to her. She put the tray down on the schoolroom table and shook her head at her forlorn cousin.

"Never mind, Susie, you old ass," she said. "Aunt Lucy will get over it."

Even this only slightly sympathetic approach was too much for Susan. "Oh, Midge," she gulped, "I wish I was dead!"

"*You* should worry," said Midge. "Aunt Lucy has written to that school."

"Midge, no!"

"But yes. Sat down and dashed it off. Apart from other considerations, the further I am from your bad influence the better, apparently."

"Midge, she didn't say that!" wailed Susan.

"She did," said Midge. "I've never known Aunt Lucy to be so incensed by anything. Of course, she does fly off the handle a bit now and then, I admit, but if Miss Plum could see the funny side of this, why not Aunt Lucy? Normally she does, but she seems to be in some sort of a flap about your character. Apparently Miss Plum warned her that you're the type who tells lies to attract attention, and of course Aunt Lucy denied it hotly and staked her life on it that you never told even the mildest fib. And now of course she's had to eat her words."

Susan was speechless. At last she gasped, "Miss Plum said that about *me*? But where on earth could she get that impression? I've hardly spoken two words to her except to thank her for the picture and the party and everything, and I've certainly never told her a lie."

"Well, that was the little character-sketch of you she gave Aunt Lucy, it seems."

"Besides," said Susan, getting more indignant the more she thought of this injustice, "I still haven't told any lies. You saw the watches in the chest of drawers yourself, and Bill—what did Bill say?" she demanded.

Midge looked a little embarrassed. "Bill," she said, "just sat there tapping his forehead—*you* know."

"Yes," said Susan grimly, "as if I were potty. *I* know."

"Oh, well," said Midge uncomfortably, "there's your dinner."

"Midge," said Susan as Midge walked to the door, "I'm terribly sorry about that school. But I'll do something—I'll——"

"Oh, ducky," said Midge quickly, "*don't* do anything more, there's an angel. And don't worry. Something'll turn up——"

She shut the door and Susan turned to her tray. "How do they think I can eat dinner when I'm so upset?" she thought. But there was some delicious-looking fish—halibut, she thought—with egg sauce over it and mashed potatoes, and in spite of her very real distress she managed to eat most of it. And she ate the apple-tart too— she didn't want Aunt Lucy to think that she was sulking.

Charlotte popped her head in. "Aunt Lucy

says you may come to the pictures if you like," she said.

"Oh, d'you think I need, Charlotte?" said Susan. "I'd feel awful."

"No, you needn't. I think Aunt Lucy will be quite glad if you don't. Just at the moment I don't think she could bear the sight of you."

"Oh, Charlotte!" said Susan.

"She'll get over it," said Charlotte, as Midge had done. "Only we did warn you not to say anything to her, didn't we? Well, never mind, it's done now. Cheer up. Mrs. Taylor will give you your tea if we're not back."

"Oh, I can wait till you come," said Susan.

She sat listening to the sounds of departure— doors banging, Midge looking for her hat and demanding loudly who had taken it, then everybody looking for it, to a crescendo of shouts, advice and recrimination; however, she must have found it because she was wearing it when she looked in on Susan to say good-bye. And then she clattered downstairs and there were more shouts and exclamations and the front door slammed.

"They all came to see me," Susan thought forlornly, watching them stumping up Tollgate Road through the snow, "except Bill. I never, *never* would have thought it of Bill——"

She went to her room to fetch a book, but she didn't even open it, just sat gazing morosely at the fire, brooding on her stupidity and the straits into which her interference had landed everyone. She thought over all that had happened and how she wished that she had kept quiet in the drawing-room! Suddenly she sat up and said to herself, "Now that's a funny thing! In the drawing-room I never said anything about the watches being *smuggled*—only that we had seen some in the chest of drawers! And yet Miss Plum immediately assumed that they had been smuggled! And talked all that rot about trembling coming through the Customs. She *must* know something about them, and I'll go next door this minute and look for clues——" And then she remembered how dark it was next door and how creepy. "And the rats——" and she shuddered and quickly picked up her book and opened it. But she couldn't read—all she could think of was Midge going off to this school, and Aunt Lucy's opinion of her as somebody who told lies to attract attention, and Bill's desertion of her. "If they won't believe what I say, I'll just have to find out more," she thought, and, trembling in every limb, she got up and went downstairs, put on her Wellington boots and big coat and a scarf, found a torch and sought out Chang. "Come along, Chang," she said, prising him off the hot-water tank in the kitchen, "you can come and keep me company, and chase the rats away."

CHAPTER TEN

SUSAN IN DANGER

Susan squeezed through the basement window, and her imagination became, as Midge might have put it, more and more inflamed. She crept up the basement stairs, and as she stood at the foot of the stairs by the front door, huddled against the wall, looking up into the gloom above and listening, every creak became a pistol-shot, every stirring of the wind about the draughty old house became a whispering of ghosts, every rustle of a dead leaf across the floors was a scampering of rats. As for Chang, thought Susan, a lot of good he was, because he had just prowled off on his own the moment they had come into the house. "Oh, well," thought Susan, "it's no good standing here. I'd better go upstairs." She wondered whether to use her torch—the horror of shining it on to a rat! But if she fell over something in the dark and killed herself? Oh, well, if she did *that*, she thought, wallowing a little in self-pity, then they'd be sorry. By this time her eyes had become accustomed to the gloom, and she realised that sufficient light was filtering round the boards and shutters of the windows to let her see well enough; so holding her torch ready to throw at rat or ghostly intruder, she ran upstairs and stopped, panting, at the door of the little room to the back of the top floor. The room was dark. Susan switched on her torch and the beam of light went exploring round the bare walls. The chest of drawers was still standing in the middle of the floor, in the wall beyond it was the door of a cupboard. There was nothing else in the room at all. The paint was dirty and chipped, the wallpaper, which had once been a pretty affair of pink roses, was faded and marked where pictures had hung; in one corner a long strip was torn and hung down forlornly. Only the floor, Susan noticed, had recently been swept. "Well," thought Susan, "I don't know what I expected, but there are no clues here. All I can do now is to hang about until the men come for the chest again and tackle them." At the thought of tackling two large and probably hostile furniture removers Susan felt quite faint. And at that moment she heard a sound—a sound different from the creaking and rustlings of the old house, a sound like—like the opening of a door. Susan stood petrified. The men had come!

But if they had come, it was immediately obvious that they were already here in the very room with her. There was another rattle of a handle, a door squeaked, Susan came to life again and leapt out of the room; she switched off her torch and got her eye to the crack of the door.

There was a footstep, a click, and the room was flooded with light. Susan blinked, and very nearly gasped—walking across the room was Miss Pershore.

Through the crack, Susan had an excellent view of her. She went straight to the little chest of drawers, and kneeling on the ground, opened the bottom drawer and began quickly to transfer the rows of watches into a small bag which she had with her.

Susan's heart leaped with joy. "I've got proof! I've got proof!" she exulted inwardly. "Maybe *now* they'll believe me——!"

And then in her impulsive way, she did something really silly. For instead of creeping quietly downstairs and telephoning Bill's friend Joe, or enlisting the help of Uncle Charles, she went bounding back into the room shouting dramatically, "Red-handed! I've caught you red-handed!"

Miss Pershore looked up at Susan with narrowed eyes.

For a moment it seemed as though she were again going to brazen things out, but then she gave a short, and extremely unpleasant, laugh and sat back on her heels. "So you're still poking your nose into other people's business, are you?" she said in a really very disagreeable voice.

"Yes," said Susan smugly. "And I've caught you red-handed. It's no good denying it this time. They'll believe me now. I've got all the proof we need."

Miss Pershore looked at her with cold dislike. Then she jumped to her feet and thrust her hand into her suit pocket. "Get over there away from that door," she snapped. "I've got a gun."

Susan almost gave at the knees. She glanced at the ominous bulge in the pocket and quickly glanced away again. For the first time it dawned on her that she had been rather foolhardy bursting in on Miss Plum like that, but she had been so thrilled at catching her actually handling the watches. . . .

"What," she began, and was horrified at the high, terrified squeak that came out instead of a voice. Then she recovered herself a little and went on, "What are you going to do with me?"

"Oh, I don't know, you pest of a child," said Miss Pershore furiously. "The game's up now, I suppose, and obviously *I* must get away before you go running to dear Lucia with your story. Why, why, *why* did you have to come blundering back here *again*? Nobody believed your story."

"They'll believe me now," said Susan, a little more stoutly.

"Oh, I realise that all right," said Miss Pershore. "It was a pity you couldn't mind your own business."

"And then what would you have done?" said Susan indignantly. "Gone on smuggling?"

"Well, naturally," said Miss Pershore. "And I wish you wouldn't keep saying *smuggling* like that as if I leapt ashore with a keg of brandy on my back."

Susan opened her mouth to say that brandy or watches, on her back or among her puppets, what difference did it make, when she had the sense to realise that that would involve Bill. She said instead, "You're a smuggler if you smuggle, and *you* smuggled those watches in the chest of drawers."

Miss Pershore said angrily, "How did you *find* those watches? To think that you've only been in the place—how long is it? A week? A week, and you have to come poking your nose in here. What made you come into this empty house anyway?"

"I came after my cat the first time," said Susan.

"Your cat!" said Miss Pershore.

"I would have found you out sooner or later," said Susan, trying to put a bold face on it. "You and your gang——"

"Oh, do stop talking in that stupid melodramatic way," said Miss Pershore. "Do I look like someone in a *gang*?"

"Then *you* hadn't anything to do with those people in the papers who had been caught?" said Susan.

"Naturally I hadn't," said Miss Pershore. "*I* should never have been caught. *My* scheme was quite foolproof. And if you want to know how

I did it, I brought the watches in specially prepared puppets—you didn't know *that*, little Miss Clever!"

Susan said nothing.

"If I had my car I brought them in the petrol tank—no obvious false compartments for me, the petrol tank was specially made to hold two gallons of petrol and the rest of the space held watches. You didn't find *that* out either——"

Susan burst out, "How can you talk like that, as if it was something to be proud of! How *could* you? It isn't as if you were poor and needed the money—you're rich anyway."

"My poor child, you don't think the dividends from the paltry thousands that my father left me are sufficient to pay for my clothes, my pictures, my jewels, all my lovely things? For my servants, my car, my flat in Paris? These things cost money. Naturally I had to supplement my income. So I worked out my little scheme for smuggling the watches into the country and organised my plan for distributing them and went on living my normal life."

Such wickedness left Susan gasping. "And, and," she stuttered, "and all that time you were living a lie, a whole lot of lies in fact, and you had the cheek to say that *I* told lies!"

"I had to say that, you little fool," said Miss Pershore, "in case you repeated the story about seeing me disappear into the cupboard."

"Of course," said Susan, "the cupboard, the day of the party! Well, you needn't have bothered," she added shortly, "because I had forgotten all about it."

"But you see how conveniently my little preliminary work came in when you produced the next preposterous story?"

"What were you doing in the cupboard?" said Susan.

"Oh, you're not even intelligent," said Miss Pershore in disgust, "haven't you realised it yet? There's a communicating door between the two houses. I discovered that after I had bought my house. Once the houses were occupied by two sisters who were very devoted to each other, and they had the door made. What with a furniture store next door and a communicating door for easy access, it wasn't difficult to work out a plan for distributing my watches without involving me at all."

"You *would* have been annoyed if some real Ivor Williams men had taken your chest of drawers full of watches one day."

"Why should they?" said Miss Pershore. "There is no furniture on this floor. No, it was a nice, tidy, simple little method, my part in which would never have been discovered if you could only have been persuaded to mind your own business, you tiresome child."

"You're a wicked woman," said Susan, "and

I'm sorry I ate those chocolates you gave me or I'd have given them back, and I hope you're very uncomfortable in prison."

"*I'm* not going to prison," said Miss Pershore, "I'm going to Paris. I'll have to get away at once, that's obvious. It's a very great nuisance that you have ruined my business, but I'll think of another good racket when I get safely out of the country. It means leaving most of my nice things behind, and I'll never forgive you for that—but I can take my jewellery, and of course a good deal of my money is in Paris anyway and——" She glanced at her watch, thinking aloud. "There's a plane leaves Northolt about eight o'clock—I've caught it often, the Customs know me well, I'll put my jewellery in the puppets, *so* convenient—I'll get that plane very comfortably."

"You certainly won't," said Susan, "for I shall tell the police."

"I know, that's the nuisance of you, you little pest. What *shall* I do with you? I can't take you with me; I can't leave you in my own house—whatever would Cook and Ellen think? I suppose I shall have to tie you up and leave you here—so sordid," said Miss Pershore in a vexed voice. "But that will give me time to get away."

Susan glanced quickly round her and made a slight movement towards the door. She wasn't nearly quick enough. Miss Pershore snapped,

"Stand still!" and poked the bulge in her pocket towards her again. All Susan's terror, which had been more or less overcome by her moral indignation, leaped up again. She swallowed the sick lump at the back of her throat, and licked dry lips. She stood very still. "Do you imagine that I told you all my little secrets so that you could run with them to the police?" said Miss Pershore. "I rather liked telling them to someone at last. Someone who couldn't repeat them." Susan swallowed again at those sinister words. "Take the belt off your coat," Miss Pershore ordered, "and give it to me."

Susan did so. "What are you going to do with that?" she said in rather a croaky voice.

"Tie you up," said Miss Pershore. "You don't think I carry a suitable length of clothes-rope about with me, do you? And don't try any tricks. Remember I have a gun."

Susan had rather hoped that the tying up would present some difficulties to Miss Pershore. It didn't at all. She bound Susan's arms behind her back extremely efficiently and so tightly that the belt bit into her wrists.

"Now you're more or less helpless," said Miss Pershore with satisfaction. "Lie down and I'll tie your legs together with your scarf——" Susan did so. She did manage to land one fairly vicious kick on Miss Pershore's ankle. Miss Pershore looked at her savagely. "If you tear my stockings," she said, "I really shall be cross with you!"

It was only when Miss Pershore had propped her against the wall that Susan noticed that the bulge seemed to have gone. "Did you not have a gun at all?" she gasped.

"Of course I didn't have a gun," said Miss Pershore, patting her empty pocket, "what *do* you take me for?"

Susan was so angry that she had let herself be fooled, that if Miss Pershore's legs had only been within reach she would have kicked her beautiful stockings to ribbons.

"Well," said Susan, with a good attempt at bravado, "it's perfectly silly tying me up here, for the minute the others get back from the pictures they'll start to look for me, and the first place they'll look will be in this house."

"Oh, no, they won't," said Miss Pershore shaking her head at Susan in a superior sort of way. "For I shall leave a little note for dear Lucia, telling her that I've carried you off to the ballet. It will look like a very pretty gesture of forgiveness on my part for all the rude things you said about me this morning. I don't know when they'll start to look for you—if ever."

Susan felt so sick with terror that something of it, she was sure, must appear on her face; and she didn't want this horrible woman to see it. She lifted up her chin and glared at her. She opened her mouth and with all the power of her lungs shrieked: "Help!"

"Be *quiet*, you little fool," said Miss Pershore furiously. She felt in Susan's pockets for a handkerchief and with that and one of her own she began to gag Susan.

Susan tried to bite her, but without success. "What's going to happen to me?" she mumbled.

"Quite frankly, you horrible child, I don't care what happens to you," said Miss Pershore. "*How* I wish you had minded your own business!"

"You couldn't wish it more than I do," thought Susan as Miss Pershore tied the gag efficiently and painfully. Then Miss Pershore calmly continued to transfer the watches from the chest of drawers into her little bag. "I don't want to leave *you* any souvenirs," she said. "How did you stumble on the watches in the chest of drawers at all?"

Susan glared at her over her gag, "'i,' 'o,'" she said.

"Oh," Miss Pershore suddenly gasped, "they were *ticking*! How stupid I was to wind them up! A clumsy fool of a Customs man dropped one of my boxes and I wound all that lot to make sure that there were none damaged. I'd sent all the others safely away. And I suppose you heard the ticking."

Susan continued to glare at her with hatred; it was all that she could do. She hoped desperately that Miss Pershore would leave the light on, but it was hardly likely, really, that she'd leave a light to shine round the cracks in the shutters and betray her. Off went the light, and off went Miss Pershore into the cupboard. The cupboard door clicked shut. More faintly the inner door clicked shut. Miss Pershore was gone, and Susan was alone.

"I don't care what she says," she thought, "they'll start looking for me sometime—perhaps to-night, certainly to-morrow . . . they'll find me all right. . . . I'll be hungry, perhaps, but that's nothing. . . . I'll be all right. A wee bit cold, maybe, but I'll be all right . . . I do wish Chang had stayed with me . . . he would have kept the rats away . . . no, *no*, NO, if I start thinking about rats I'll go completely potty . . . if I make a noise they'll keep away . . . but how can I, when I'm gagged. . . . *Why* didn't I mind my own business?" She listened; the old house creaked and rustled. "When I was little," she thought, "and afraid to go up all those shadowy stairs to bed at home I used to sing hymns . . . I can't sing when I'm gagged . . . but maybe I can hum."

And valiantly, desperately, stopping every now and then to listen fearfully, Susan started to hum, *Hark the Herald Angels Sing*. . . .

CHAPTER ELEVEN

CHANG SAVES THE DAY

TOWARDS six o'clock, the others got off the bus and came crunching home through the crisp snow. They had seen a very good film, they had had tea in a very grand hotel and they should all have enjoyed themselves very much. They *had* enjoyed themselves, in a way, but each felt inwardly that it would have been much more fun if Susan had been there, and that all this business had cast a gloom over the afternoon, although none of them said as much in so many words. Aunt Lucy had recovered her temper and was feeling worried and unhappy about the whole thing. She had been much too severe, she thought, but really, how could she have laughed off those terrible lies? And what was going to become of Susan if this sort of thing went on? She was imaginative, Aunt Lucy knew that, but there was a difference between genuine imagination and this weaving of fantastic nonsense about their own friends. She sighed—and realised that Bill was asking her something.

"What did you say, Bill?" she said, rousing herself.

Bill said patiently, for the third time, actually,

"Aunt Lucy, d'you mind if I pop into the police station for a minute?"

"What on earth for?" said Aunt Lucy, glancing up at the West Wichwood police station, which they were passing at that moment.

"I just want to have a word with my friend Joe, if he has come on duty again," said Bill.

"Yes, all right," said Aunt Lucy. "It's too cold to hang about waiting for you, we'll go on and you can catch us up."

Bill caught them up half-way along Wichwood Common. He whispered to Midge, "Joe's coming down to the house as soon as he can—in about half an hour."

Midge gaped at him. "What's Joe coming down for?"

"'Sh," whispered Bill, making signs at Aunt Lucy's back, "those watches in the chest of drawers. He's going to have a look at the house next door."

"Of course," said Midge and giggled. For one awful moment she had visualised Joe arriving with handcuffs and Black Maria to take Susan off to prison.

When they reached the house, their father and Miss Bracken, the dispenser, were busy coping with the six o'clock surgery; and the note from Miss Pershore was lying in the hall.

"Oh, thank goodness!" cried Aunt Lucy, when she had read it. "That *is* an olive branch. Thank goodness she's not offended with Susan—it would have been too uncomfortable having her disliking Susan all the time. Not without cause, though, I must say. What's the matter, Bill? You don't look too pleased."

Bill was reading the note with a worried and rather puzzled expression. He jumped a little. "Oh, it's nothing, Aunt Lucy," he said quickly. "Only the show Susan and I were going to give to-night—it won't be any good without Susan. And Miss Pershore, of course, to put half a crown in the collection."

"Really, Bill," said Aunt Lucy. But she was half-laughing, so relieved and thankful she felt, that the horrid affair of the morning was turning out to be a very small storm in a teacup after all. She said, "Perhaps you could have the show after they come back from the ballet. The ballet finishes fairly early, and after all it is Hogmanay."

"Oh, thank you, Aunt Lucy," said Bill but he still sounded as if he were thinking of something else.

"Come along, Charlotte," said Aunt Lucy, "and help me with the supper. You set the table."

Midge was going through the house calling, "Chang, Chang, Chang. That cat's gone again," she said rather unnecessarily, coming back to the sitting-room.

"I expect he's next door," said Bill.

"It has a fatal fascination for him," said Midge. "It must be the delicious smell of rat."

"Not fatal, I hope," said Bill. "Let's go and get him before Susan gets back. I shouldn't like him to be lost when she comes home."

"Okay," said Midge. "We'd better make sure he *is* there and not really lost. I'll get torches."

Bill went into the dining-room where Charlotte was laying the table.

"Charlotte," he said, "if Joe comes before I'm back, bring him next door, will you?"

"Now look here, Bill," said Charlotte, "we've had quite enough bother about that beastly house next door. You keep out of it—the house *and* the bother."

"Well, Midge and I are just going to get Chang," said Bill, "and I must show Joe the watches in the chest of drawers. I mean, they're real enough, *Midge* saw them too."

"They won't *still* be there, for goodness' sake," said Charlotte.

"I can show him the chest," said Bill. "Be a sport, Charlotte—remember Joe's promotion."

Joe's promotion was a cause dear to the hearts of all the Carmichaels. "All right," said Charlotte. "How do we get in?"

"There's a window at the back with some loose boards—you can't miss it. But we'll probably be back before Joe comes. 'Bye!"

"Put on a coat," called Charlotte.

Bill muttered, but put on his coat. Midge was ready. "Just going to look for Chang," they called out to Aunt Lucy, busy in the kitchen, and went out by the back door. They sped down the garden to the hole in the fence, and through the snow-covered ruin of the garden next door.

As they struggled through the window Bill panted, "I hope Joe will get through this window."

"Joe?" said Midge. "Is Joe coming?"

"Sometime," said Bill. "He and I are investigating this thing about the watches in the chest of drawers."

Midge smiled to herself. "Oh, yes," she said gravely. "'S'matter of fact," she went on, "in the general upset I'd forgotten that Susan and I really did see watches in the chest of drawers. She didn't make that up. Why on earth she had to go dragging Miss Plum into it, I can't think. At least I can of course—it was to rescue us all from the effects of Miss Plum's bad influence on Aunt Lucy. Poor old Susie—if *only* she would mind her own business and not insist on rescuing everybody—she has pretty well wrecked me. And Bill, what on *earth* made her say you found watches *inside* a puppet?"

Bill said uncomfortably, thankful for the darkness, "Never mind about that now. Where d'you think Chang will be? Just generally on the prowl?"

"Last time," said Midge, "we eventually found him fast asleep on an upholstered chair in a room on the ground floor. Chang likes his comfort—I'll show you."

They went upstairs, but there was no Chang on the chair in the room on the ground floor. Bill shone his torch round the sheeted furniture. Midge called softly, "Chang, Chang, Chang!"

"Well, he doesn't seem to be here," said Bill and went out to the hall. Then he stopped, "Midge," he said, "do *you* hear a funny noise?"

They listened. Midge said, "Well, I *thought* I heard someone singing, but it must be outside."

Bill went a little way up the stairs and listened again. "It's not singing, it's humming," he said, "and I don't believe it's outside. I believe it's upstairs."

"It c-c-can't be," quavered Midge, not feeling quite so brave.

They listened again. There was a faint but distinct sound of *Once in Royal David's City* being hummed.

"Midge, come on," said Bill. "This is queer," and he sounded frightened.

"Don't you think we should wait for Joe?" said Midge. "I mean I know there aren't any such things, but it might be a ghost."

"What good would Joe be, if it was a ghost?" said Bill. "Besides, a ghost wouldn't hum *Once in Royal David's City*. Come on!"

As Bill was by this time nearly at the first floor, Midge felt that the only thing to do was to hurry after him. They paused on the first landing and listened again. Strains of *God Rest You Merry Gentlemen* came faintly down to them.

"It's upstairs," said Bill.

"P'raps it's from the room where we found the chest of drawers," said Midge, "but who can it be?"

They ran upstairs. The humming was quite loud now. "That's the room," whispered Midge and waved her torch at the door. The humming stopped and they heard a strangled sort of groan. Midge swallowed and grabbed Bill by the arm. Slowly they advanced to the door of the little room and shone their torches within. In a corner against the wall was Susan, gagged and bound. Across her knees lay Chang, head up, ears pricked, spitting at them.

Midge said stupidly, "It's Susan. But Susan's at the ballet!"

"Mm, m-m-m-m," said Susan.

"Oh, Susan, *darling*!" cried Midge and darted towards her and began to unfasten the gag. In the light of Bill's torch Susan jerked her head towards the ceiling and looked upwards.

"What is it?" said Bill, shining his torch upwards. "Gosh, a light! Where's the switch?" He located the switch, and the little room was flooded with light.

"I *can't* get this knot undone," wailed Midge, "I can't."

"Here, let me," said Bill, pulling his knife out of his pocket, and cutting the knot in the handkerchief. He cut off a bit of hair too, but nobody cared about that.

Susan worked her tongue round her dry mouth and waggled her jaw. "That was awful," she said, "worse than the dentist." She beamed at her cousins. "Am I glad to see you!" she said. "How did you know I was here?"

"Well, of course we didn't know you were here," said Midge, "we thought you were at the ballet. We were looking for Chang."

"For Chang, the dear wee fellow!" said Susan. "So that's how you found me. She forgot Chang! I'd have gone dotty but for Chang—I can't tell you what a comfort it was when he came back and sat on me—cosy, too." Bill was hacking away at the knots round Susan's wrists. "Bill!" Susan suddenly shrieked. "I've just remembered! That's the belt of my good coat!"

"Was, you mean," said Bill, holding up the severed ends of belt.

"Oh, *look* at your poor wrists!" said Midge, as Susan slowly brought her stiff arms in front of her. Midge began to rub her numb hands very gingerly to bring some feeling back into them. "Who did this to you, Susie?" she said.

"Well," said Susan with a reproachful glance

at Bill, "I know you won't believe me, but it was Miss Plum."

There was a confused noise below, like a young bull getting in among the furniture. "That'll be Joe," said Bill. He darted to the head of the stairs. "*Joe!*" he yelled. "Come up here, quick!" There was a thunder of feet, and Joe, followed by Charlotte, arrived.

"Susan!" shrieked Charlotte.

"Now then, now then," said Joe, "what's all this?"

Midge giggled. "Oh, Joe, stop pretending to be a proper policeman," she said.

Bill was cutting the scarf away from Susan's ankles. "Tell them, Susie," said Bill.

"Not if you're going to start denying everything again," said Susan in a hurt voice.

"Oh, you ass, I had to do that," said Bill impatiently. "I told you to shut up and you wouldn't—you went blurting everything out. I saw Miss Plum pass the window, and if I hadn't said I didn't know what you were talking about, you would have blurted it out to Miss Plum herself, and then Miss Plum would have been off before Joe could catch her."

Susan cried, "What's the time?"

"It's seven o'clock, miss," said Joe.

"Well, hurry, hurry!" cried Susan. "She's catching a plane for Paris at Northolt at eight, and she's a smuggler of watches all right, and when I caught her right here in this very house she knew she couldn't bluff it out any longer, so she tied me up and took the watches out of the chest of drawers and went."

Joe, red with excitement, said, "You'd better come up to the station with me, miss, and tell all this to the sergeant. Can you walk?"

Susan struggled to her feet and immediately collapsed again. "No," she said, "my legs won't hold me."

"I'll phone for a car," said Joe. "Can I use your phone, young Bill?"

"You'd be quicker phoning from Miss Pershore's," said Susan airily. "Through that press—cupboard."

She couldn't help feeling rather like a conjurer as they exclaimed at the communicating door. Bill and Joe disappeared to find the telephone. Charlotte and Midge helped Susan to her feet again and supported her as she took a few staggering steps.

"The *horrible* woman, the *horrible* woman!" Midge kept repeating. "If it hadn't been for Chang I don't know *when* we'd have found you—you might have been dead!"

"I'd have been dead from starvation anyway," said Susan. "I nearly am now!"

"I'll go home and grab something for you," said Charlotte, but at that moment Joe and Bill came back.

"Come along now, miss," said Joe, "the car's coming down. You come along and tell your story to the sergeant."

"I must come," said Midge, "and give my evidence."

"I'm coming," said Bill.

"I'm certainly coming," said Charlotte.

"I don't see that you need come, Charlotte," said Bill, "you weren't really in it."

"I helped to rescue her, didn't I?" said Charlotte indignantly. "I can tell them how Joe and I found the poor little soul——"

"You'd better *all* come," said Joe, and they trooped down through Miss Pershore's exquisite house, which made them feel rather peculiar, while the cook and the elegant parlourmaid peered out at them with scared and indignant faces from behind the kitchen door.

CHAPTER TWELVE

NEW YEAR RESOLUTIONS

THEY didn't get a very good welcome from Aunt Lucy when they came home again.

"Really, children," she said, "where have you been? Suddenly there's not one of you to be found in the house—I look out of the window and there you all are piling into a police—*Susan!* Susan!" she said, gazing at her dirty, dishevelled, untidy-haired niece, "I thought you were at the ballet?"

"No, Aunt Lucy," said Susan, "I was lying bound and gagged next door."

"And as for you, Charlotte," went on Aunt Lucy, "I ask you to set the table and you just calmly go off in the middle—*what* did you say, Susan?"

"I said," said Susan, "that I was lying bound and gagged in the empty house next door."

Aunt Lucy burst out, "Now look here, Susan, I might as well tell you here and now that these stories have got to *stop*. Nobody thinks it's funny, nobody thinks it's clever, nobody——"

"Aunt Lucy," Charlotte interrupted before Aunt Lucy could work herself up any further, "it's quite true."

"The other thing I said this morning was true too," said Susan.

"We've just been up at the police station telling the police, and they're going to have her stopped before she gets the plane and my friend Joe's frightfully hopeful about his promotion—if he passes his exams as well, of course. Even the sergeant seemed quite impressed, eventually," said Bill.

"It would be nice if Joe got promoted *above* that sergeant," said Midge, "because he was inclined to be a bit snooty at first about our story."

Aunt Lucy said very quietly, "Now look, will one of you, *one* of you, please tell *me* your story."

They all immediately burst into speech.

"But you *know* it, Aunt Lucy!"

"Well, you wouldn't believe me, but she really is a smuggler and——"

"I know she was a friend of yours, Aunt Lucy, but she left Susie to *rot*, and I don't think *that's* very friendly——"

"——the only nice thing about her was her puppets, and I'm even a bit off puppets at the moment after what she did to Susie——"

"And Chang, Aunt Lucy, really he was sweet, because the sergeant said that he was really the hero of the day, and Chang purred like anything and——"

Aunt Lucy clapped her hands to her ears very

melodramatically. "*Stop!*" she shouted. In the comparative lull that followed she said, "Susan, will you tell me the whole story and the rest of us will sit down quietly and listen!"

"Yes, Aunt Lucy," said Susan, "I will. The only thing is, I'm terribly hungry, quite faint really, and I was wondering about supper——"

"Supper!" shrieked Aunt Lucy. "I've got a cheese pudding in the oven!" and she ran to the kitchen.

In the end, they decided to have the story over supper, and then the doctor could hear it too, and that would save going over it all again, although actually nobody seemed averse to going over every detail at least twenty times.

Dr. Carmichael and Aunt Lucy were stunned and horrified to hear that Miss Pershore had indeed been leading a double life.

"From what she told me," said Susan, "and of course she only told me because she thought that she'd be safely out of the country before I could tell anyone else, she had got this smuggling racket pretty well organised. She brought the watches over from Paris."

"And to think," murmured Aunt Lucy, "that I went with her to Paris once! Probably she was smuggling *that* time!"

"Probably you brought the watches through the Customs, my dear Lucy," said Uncle Charles.

This was a very disturbing idea for Aunt Lucy.

So Susan hurried on, "The police seemed to think that she established herself as a regular traveller with her puppets until she was quite well known to the Customs' officials and above suspicion, and then she started bringing the watches through."

"And where did the chest of drawers come in?" said Aunt Lucy.

"Well, she had other people working for her too; she packed the watches into the chest of drawers, and two of her men pretending to be furniture men came and took it to the dealer or the shop or whoever it was who was going to sell them—the police are going to look into that angle —where the Ivor Williams van came from and everything."

Midge said, "I wonder why she bothered about all that, why not just take them to the shop herself?"

"Well, I don't know of course," said Charlotte, "but she had a reputation to preserve, remember, and I should think it would be to avoid any direct contact with the shop, which might look suspicious."

"I'll never get over it," said Aunt Lucy. "I don't feel that I'll ever be able to trust anyone again. It doesn't seem right that anyone so dishonest should be so charming on the surface, and have such a love of beautiful things. It quite puts me off ballet and all the things she liked."

"That's perfectly ridiculous," said Uncle

Charles. "You can like and enjoy books and paintings and music and beautiful jewels and furniture without taking to crime in order to have them!"

He went on in this strain for some time, but Susan had stopped listening. She kicked Midge's ankle under the table and made expressive faces at her, and when Uncle Charles paused to take a bite of pudding she said, "Aunt Lucy, about that dancing school where you were going to send Midge——"

"That school!" said Aunt Lucy, "I wouldn't touch it with a barge-pole!"

"Now that *is* illogical," said Uncle Charles severely. "But I think, as indeed I've thought all along, it would be much better for Midge to stay on at St. Ronan's. She must keep up her dancing, but she can get a lot of pleasure and profit out of her dancing without making it her career. It's not a bit of use trying to push somebody into that kind of life unless they are madly keen."

Midge and Susan beamed at each other.

"What about this puppet show you promised us, Bill?" Uncle Charles went on. "It's Hogmanay, and my patients will have to get on without me for the rest of the evening."

"Oh, would you like to see it?" said Bill. "Oh, then we'll do it, won't we, Susan?"

"Sure," said Susan.

At this point the telephone rang, and Uncle

Charles groaned. "I suppose my patients just won't get on without me," he muttered. But it wasn't a patient, it was the police, to say that Miss Pershore had been taken into custody at the airport and did Dr. Carmichael wish to prefer a charge against her for assault on the young lady? And after Uncle Charles had made sure that Miss Pershore would go to trial anyway for her smuggling activities—sufficient evidence of *that* having been found on her and in her house—he decided not to press the charge about Susan.

"Oh, thank goodness!" said Aunt Lucy. "Naturally, I didn't want her to get off scot-free, but she was our neighbour and friend for over a year."

"Aunt Lucy," said Midge, "*could* we stay up to see the New Year in this year? We never have, and we ought to have a special celebration after to-day and——"

"Oh, I don't know," Aunt Lucy said doubtfully. "Susan ought to get off to bed early after her ordeal."

While it sounded delightfully important to have had an ordeal, Susan was forced to admit that she didn't feel a penny the worse for it, except that her wrists were still bruised and cut, but Uncle Charles had promised to put something on them to help that, so Aunt Lucy gave in and there was great jubilation.

"Well, come on, then," she said. "I'll clear

away—it's the turn of Midge and Bill to wash up because Charlotte helped me before supper, even if she did go away in the middle."

Charlotte said that she would wash up instead of Bill so that he could get on with the puppets; so Susan and Bill went off to the schoolroom and made their preparations; and the show was a tremendous success, and the collection came to six-and-twopence.

"I think that's jolly good," said Susan afterwards, counting it for the fifth time. "But," she added sadly, "it's a long way off eight pounds. And the police didn't mention a word about a reward for catching Miss Plum, did they?"

Charlotte said, "Susie, maybe you could have got damages for what Miss Plum did to you."

"Bother!" said Susan. "It's too late now. We should have thought of that sooner, and now Uncle Charles has said he won't bring a charge against her for tying me up. Oh, bother!" And then suddenly she had a brainwave. "That picture she gave me, that drawing! *I* don't want her old picture, although I must say I liked it— I'll sell it!"

"Let's *all* sell our pictures!" said Charlotte. "We'll tell the people at the exhibition that we want the money back, and surely we'll get eight pounds for the lot and we can buy a train for Bill?"

Bill was almost overcome by this generosity.

But when Aunt Lucy heard about it she had an even better idea. "*I'll* give you eight pounds for the sketches," she said, "because they're too nice to sell back. And I'll hang them on the stair—I've been wanting something for that wall for a long time—and they'll be a constant reminder to me of my foolishness. For I have been foolish, trying to force you children into tastes and enthusiasms rather than let you come to them naturally —as I know you will, when you are ready for them, for already you don't like the second-rate. *You* recognised that Miss Pershore was shoddy and I didn't."

"Aunt Lucy," said Bill, "I don't think you should *brood* about Miss Plum too much, because she's not worth it, and *if* I get my train, which I must say would be absolutely super, would you mind if I gave the puppets to Susan because she likes them better than I do really, and I can help her to make a little stage for them?"

"Oh, Bill!" said Susan.

It was almost the end of the old year. It was terribly thrilling seeing the New Year in, Susan and Midge quite agreed, only not very much *happened*, did it? Midge yawned. Susan yawned. But then twelve o'clock struck, and the bells pealed out on the wireless, and they wished each other a happy New Year and sang *A Guid New Year tae Ane and A'* and ate shortbread and drank ginger wine, and things livened up a bit. Then the bell rang, and the "first foot" arrived, the traditional dark man, carrying coal and bread and money, and, what was more interesting to the family, a box of chocolates and a box of crystallised fruits.

And then Aunt Lucy shoo'ed the family off to bed. "Good-night, Susan," said Uncle Charles, "and a happy, happy New Year to you. It has been an exciting beginning to your holidays with us, but we can't always promise to provide such thrills—from now on, I *hope*, you'll have to make do with more ordinary things like visits to the Zoo and the Tower and Madame Tussaud's."

"But I'll love *that*," said Susan.

"Off you go, all of you," said Aunt Lucy after she had kissed them, "and let me get my New Year resolutions written. Number One—Mind your own business."

"Ugh, Aunt Lucy," said Susan, shaking her head at her sadly, "it's no good. *I*'ve made that one every New Year's Day for as long as I can remember!"

THE END